Cross The Veil And Near Me Dwell

WRITTEN BY: MONICA JO CARUSI

ILLUSTRATIONS AND COVER ART BY: JORDAN BAER

First Edition –September 2012

ISBN
978-1-4602-0447-4 (Hardcover)
978-1-4602-0445-0 (Paperback)
978-1-4602-0446-7 (eBook)

Produced by:

FriesenPress
Suite 300 – 852 Fort Street
Victoria, BC, Canada V8W 1H8

www.friesenpress.com

Distributed to the trade by The Ingram Book Company

Table of Contents

TABLE OF CONTENTS

Much gratitude and thanks to Lisa, Eric and Michelle. Your enthusiasm and encouragement for my first manuscript was truly a blessing.

Introduction

Secrets and the revelation of those secrets are the lifeblood of all good stories. To be responsible for knowledge of which all others are unaware is both energizing and burdensome. Secrets can sustain their holder or suck them into a swirling abyss of paranoia and fear, the only escape from which may be to lay the secret bare for all to know. Hmmm. Sustenance or swirling abyss; if those are in fact the only two options I believe, that which happens must be dependent upon the secret and its holder.

I have kept a secret for most of my life, but I haven't yet decided if it has sustained me, or led me into that abyss. I guess my life story is both unique and common and, like you, I won't know how it turns out until it's all over. But then, we all will find out in the end.

I realize that I need to add what I consider to be appropriate disclaimers at this juncture. Please understand that I, in no way, assert myself to be psychic; I don't know how to read auras and I am not a medium; at least none of these descriptors are true in the traditional sense. I have no knowledge of those gifts or how they apply to the lives of the gifted. Neither am I crazy. There is no mental illness in my medical history. Unless true logic is to be considered a psychological defect, then I may need to reconsider my mental health status. I am, in fact, so logical in my life's vision that I often fail to understand the expressive reactions of others. I do not grasp emotionally-based decisions made by people who appear to be otherwise rational. I will admit that even now this is a great mystery to me. This difficulty was especially true in my youth. Thankfully, with time and experience, I have gained wisdom and knowledge. As I have grown older, I have learned to try to empathize with others. Initially, I mimicked other people so I could fit in better or at least not stick out quite as much. I acted as if I understood how they were feeling. I did that for so long that eventually, on some level, I suppose, I could anticipate emotional reactions and project what should be my appropriate response.

Do not think that I am made of stone. My feelings have certainly been hurt in my life. Especially as a young child, I was so very sensitive, scared and shy. The problem is that logic and emotions, at least to me, are opposite cerebral functions. My early childhood was spent desperately trying to comprehend my innate logic along with the visceral emotions I neither liked nor understood. And yet those emotions were so powerful I could not move beyond them. They were paralyzing. I was scared of everything. I was terrified that someone would make fun of me, that I would make a mistake and be laughed at. I learned very early on that the adults in my family enjoyed gossiping and swapping stories about not only their children but also of the children of their own siblings. They laughed with what seemed to me to be evil glee when some aspect of someone else's child could be criticized and picked upon. I knew better than to share my thoughts or my feelings with any of them. Especially since I mostly disagreed with their concrete view of the world and of life in general, I knew that any information I had given would certainly have been fodder for their chitchat. I didn't want anyone to talk about me. I wanted desperately to hide from everything and everyone and to be left alone.

I realize now of course that this was the over-reaction of a small extremely sensitive child whose life experiences hadn't yet allowed her to develop a sense of the big picture. Of course, my family loves me and

I them. I just needed to live long enough and have enough life experience to understand. What seemed like evil glee early in life was really sisters talking, swapping stories, and interacting as sisters do. At this point, I have pretty much decided that we all just need to be around long enough to understand one another.

Thankfully, I had significant help from some really great teachers in my life. They helped me see that I was stronger (both mentally and physically) and smarter than I had been allowing myself to be. Basically, one day, I decided that I would not be scared for the rest of my days. I decided that I would stand up for myself no matter what the opposition.

How and who helped me come to this realization is the secret I have so diligently guarded throughout my life.

We all know we have family. Even if we do not know who they are, we know that somewhere there are, or were, at least two people who each provided one half of our DNA. They are called our parents, whether they raised us or not. Each of our parents had two parents and so on, and that is how our ancestral lineage is documented.

If we are lucky in our lifetime, we may get to know our parents, their parents, and their parents' parents. Most often, however, great grandparents do not live long enough within our own lifetime to be remembered as anything other than really old people who most likely smelled funny. They leave our lives on this, the physical or material plane of existence, and join our family members on what is often referred to as "the other side".

I have learned that the so-called "other side" isn't really a side at all. It is actually another plane of existence. And this is where my secret comes into play. The unique thing about me, that I have guarded so desperately all of my life, is that I not only know my parents' parents' parents; but I have spoken with their parents' parents' parents as well. You see, I have the ability to see and speak with my own ancestors as well as anyone they choose to introduce to me.

I believe Sir Isaac Newton, Julius Robert von Mayer, James Prescott Joule and Albert Einstein each spent many hours of their lives developing, working with and expanding upon the Law of Conservation of Energy, an idea I consider to be exactly on point. In fact, I often wonder if they weren't really somehow considering the afterlife when they broached the subject matter but then saw its practical application here on the material plane and ran with it. Simply put, the law states: "Energy cannot be created or destroyed, it can only be changed from one form to another."

I am amazed at how simply and elegantly it also describes the movement of each person's spirit or energy to the ethereal plane when the human body can no longer sustain its existence here on the physical or material plane.

Anyway, that is quite enough of the educational lecture. I have found I often gain a better or greater understanding of difficult concepts when the lesson comes in the form of a story. And so that is what I have done. In order to better explain my "secret", I am offering the story of my life right up to the end of my fourth grade year. From my fifth grade school year on, things got very complicated and the story would be excessively long, so I have chosen to tell you only about my life from birth to grade 4 for now.

Family and friends of family told many parts of this tale to me from "the other side". I have taken the stories as conveyed by them and woven them into a single narrative for you. I will begin by introducing you to my family members on both planes of existence. I truly hope you find them as wonderfully fascinating as I do.

Section I:
Meet The Family

Chapter I: The Ethereal Plane ("The Other Side")

Lucille had always taken pride in her personal appearance and in the appearance of her home. That is why, even on the ethereal plane, she maintained the presentation of both with great care and diligence. She herself was a thin, elderly woman who dressed in fashionable clothing of the Victorian era and carried a decorative cane in her left hand. She always wore a beautifully appropriate hat to each and every occasion she attended. Lucille was, at all times, proper in her discourse and manners; how else could a Victorian era well-bred woman behave, after all? This was who she was throughout her physical life; this is who she is in her 'afterlife', and this is who she will be until she is reborn to the material plane. And if the truth were told, this is who Lucille would very much prefer to continue to be even then.

Lucille had truly loved her home on the material plane. So much so that she had taken immense effort to recreate it as her private residence on the ethereal plane. It was an Italianate style structure that had corniced eaves and an angled bay window. She loved the Corinthian-columned porch to which she added many plants of various origins and a lovely ornate bench-style swing for relaxing whenever she wasn't performing duties as dictated by the Family Council. At this moment, however, as was often the case, Lucille was becoming very impatient. So impatient, in fact, that she began to pace the marble floor of the elaborate entranceway to her home with large flowery yet tasteful wallpaper on which she had strategically placed a great portrait of her father between two enclosed wall-mounted oil lamps. The flickering of their light danced upon his countenance so that he might seemingly judge all who entered her home.

"I will never understand how someone who has existed on the ethereal plane since the time of ancient Rome, as Gillius has, cannot yet manage to appear when called," she said aloud to no one in particular, or maybe she was discussing the matter with her father.

Abruptly, she stopped pacing the floor and closed her eyes. Clearly fighting her impatience and frustration, she willfully focused her thoughts and again spoke aloud. She demanded, "Gillius Quintus! You emerge this instant! I will leave without you; I swear I will!"

As if upon her command (although it was really just a coincidence), a swirling, purple, hazy mist opened in the doorway with the ornately carved molding and a man, somewhat shorter and decidedly heavier than Lucille came into view. He wore the formal toga of a Roman statesman and walked calmly through the mist. He entered the foyer carrying the hem of the toga draped over his arm, and beams of platinum light trailed behind him. As the hazy mist slowly dissipated, Gillius realized immediately that he must assuage an obviously annoyed Lucille.

"Hurry up Gillius!" Lucille admonished. "You are always late for everything! Wait for Gillius! Wait for Gillius! Must we always wait for Gillius? One of our own has been born and we need to greet her with the family that will raise her! The rest of the council is already there!"

"My dear Lucille," calmly replied Gillius in as soothing a tone as he had ever produced, "you know as well as I that there is no need to ever hurry. Time has no meaning here on the ethereal plane. For that matter, neither does that cane of yours. Once we pass from the material to the ethereal we are completely free from physical detriment. Why do you carry that implement?"

"Because, dear Gillius," came a sassy retort as Lucille donned her matching hat (and a rather large hat it was too), "it was part of my being on the material plane and many from our family recognize it as well as my energy. When they see me, they very much expect to see my distinctively ornate cane. Therefore," she said with finality, "it goes where I do."

"Hmmm, of course," nodded a very stately Gillius, "how silly of me. I haven't been reborn in so long I have nearly forgotten what it is like to have any change at all. For me, I guess it is this toga that family members recognize as well as my energy. I suppose I am a bit jealous of our Madeline and her chance to live again on the material plane. You ought never to repeat this, Lucille, but I must admit she is my favorite great, great, great, great, great…oh you know…grandniece. I cannot help but wonder why it is that Madeline has been reborn so soon after entering the ethereal plane. What is it that the Universal Energy could have planned for her in this new lifetime? When we discovered she was no longer on this plane, besides missing her company of course, I found myself contemplating that of all we can see and hear and understand, I find that I most wonder why we cannot see when it will be our turn to reenter the physical realm. It just happens that our energy is placed into a newly conceived child and we do not see them again until they are reborn."

"I suppose," a now calmer and thoughtful Lucille began, "that we have to accept that we simply are not meant to know the moment of our rebirth or how many lives we will live on the material plane. Besides, I do rather enjoy the surprise of it all. There is so little we do not see or cannot know here on the ethereal plane that a little uncertainty keeps us on our toes."

Gillius mused, "I heartily agree. I should also say that I truly appreciate our ability to see into the material world. I do so enjoy watching each of our family members as they grow and learn, overcoming the obstacles that have kept them in the rebirth cycle. I even like to cheer them on as they do...until they are reunited with us on this side again."

"But it was you who reminded me that time means nothing here," Lucille inquired. "Why do you say it has been so long?"

"Look at the material plane as it currently is." Gillius waved an outstretched hand and they both looked through a purple mist that suddenly lifted to reveal a crystal clear image of daily life in Rome, Italy. He changed the scene to show London, England. Then he manipulated the viewer to show life all over the world as it went on in present time.

"And now look to see back to when I last existed in the physical realm." A small gesture from Gillius and the mists swirled and shifted to show the daily life of Roman citizens just after the Common Era began. "How much has changed! How much I will have to learn. I must say I am rather looking forward to it!"

Lucille nodded her agreement. "I am also looking forward to that moment but enough of this wishful conversation for now. There is a far more important matter to attend too. We should be off to meet the newest arrival to the material plane." Lucille held out her cane in front of her and tapped once on the floor. The purple haze that allowed them to move about the ethereal realm as well as journey to the material plane reappeared in front of them.

Gillius offered Lucille an arm and into the purple shifting haze they vanished each trailed by their own brilliant colored beams of energy of platinum and silver light.

Chapter II: Josie

Family members on the material plane have the greatest impact upon us when we arrive. Its like that old adage: you only get one chance at making a first impression. It sort of sets the stage for things to come. It is funny how each of us remembers the same events differently. Of course, it is our point of view and level of understanding at any given time that shades our memories. My sister Josie and I each have remarkable powers of recall. She was just a toddler when I came to live with our family but she says she can remember it like it was yesterday. I asked Josie to put herself back into the mindset of the day I arrived, and to relive those memories for me but to relate them as if she were telling a story to a stranger. I thought you might get a better sense of our relationship that way. Of course, being the wonderful big sister she is (now), Josie was only too happy to help with this endeavor. What follows is Josie's account of that day.

"It was hot and sunny and even though the windows in the family sedan were rolled down, Dad was grouchy, our older sister, Joaney, was whining about how warm it was and the boys were punching each other across Joaney and me even though we had been strategically placed in the vehicle to permit as much separation as possible between them."

"Our little sister arrived on August 13th. When I say arrived, I don't mean in the traditional way babies arrive into families. I mean when our parents, two older brothers, older sister and I came home from a family camping trip that afternoon, she was there waiting for us. We were all tired of being in the car and of the long trip home pulling the camper behind us. We turned into the stone filled driveway to find an old, rail thin wrinkly woman, dressed all in black, waiting there with her in front of the little brick house our father had built. This really wasn't that unusual an occurrence in our family. Only Joaney, the oldest child, our oldest sister, arrived in the conventional way. The rest of us just showed up. Let me explain. Once, I overheard Mom explain to Joaney and the boys (Alvin and James) that it took them (Mom and Dad) many years to conceive their first daughter, Joaney. After she was born, it seemed that Mom could not have any more children, but they really wanted to raise a larger family, so they adopted the rest of us. Our two brothers and sister are all older. There is six years between our brother James and me, Alvin is seven years older and Joaney is fourteen years older than me. I guess Mom got the baby itch again so they adopted me, Josie. I was cute and bubbly and quite frankly the apple of my father's eye. Dad said that my eyes sparkled. I loved to hear him say that. I toddled after him whenever he was home. I was a real Daddy's girl. In fact, I got all the attention I wanted from just about everyone. I made sure of it. I could get anyone except our mother to do just about anything and I have to admit I was pretty proud of it. I knew when to giggle, when to bat my eyes, when to scream and when to cry to get someone to come running to do what I wanted, when I wanted, how I wanted it done. Mom was on to me though. She decided that I needed someone younger than me in the family, so I wouldn't get all the attention and turn into a spoiled brat. Yep, I needed someone to play with, and to learn to share with, so they adopted my little sister, Jane."

"I am not quite two years older than Jane. From the moment I met her on that bright sunny day in August, I knew she was different. I remember Dad was holding me in his arms and everyone else was standing around straining to see, when the mean looking adoption agency lady handed her over to our mother. Mom immediately cooed at the blanketed bundle in her arms, and everyone else oohed and ahhed at her. Dad said, "Look Josie, this is your new sister! You're a big sister now!" When he said it, it sounded like it should be a good thing, like I now had more standing or importance in the family. For a very brief moment, I thought, "This is great! I have someone to boss around now." And then, our eyes met and I got this sinking feeling in my stomach. I knew this girl was going to be something. I didn't know what, but I knew to the core of my being that she was going to be important. Maybe she could be even more important than me. I didn't like that feeling at all."

"I think I knew from her eyes. Eyes are supposed to be the windows to the soul. Jane's eyes were different. They didn't sparkle like mine; they penetrated, they looked right into you. It was like from the moment she saw me, she knew who I really was. As we got older Mom would say, "When Jane is watching you, you know you are being watched!" Of course, that was down the road from the moment I'm describing now; for now, I wasn't sure what to make of this situation but I was certain that being Jane's big sister was not to my advantage."

"I immediately assessed the situation. In my short life, I had learned to read people right away. Maybe, I just came with the gift of manipulation but somehow, for some reason, I could easily grasp interactions between people. I knew innately what someone needed me to give them emotionally so they would do what I wanted. I had already discovered that sometimes I had to manipulate one person to manage another. That is how I stayed in control and believe me it was a lot of work to keep Mom, Dad, my older sister and two brothers jumping to meet my wants and desires. Truthfully, though, I didn't mind it too much; really it was kind of fun to see what I could get them to do. One time, when I was still just a baby, I kept my two brothers rocking my cradle for hours. Now that was really fun. Every time they would slow down too much or stop and try to leave the room, I would scream and scream and scream until Mom made them stay put and rock me. The boys were exasperated! It was thrilling and I loved it! I just wanted to be sure they knew who was in charge. Ah well, that was one of my happier memories; I should get back to the day I promised to tell you about."

"I needed to address the situation before me. Mom was standing there holding Jane so I could see her. Looking her over, there were differences between us that I thought I could exploit. I was cute and personable. Grown-ups seemed to like my appearance. Jane had those penetrating eyes and only one eyebrow. It went right across her forehead with no break at the nose. "There is definitely something wrong with her," I thought. "Ha, ha! Looks funny!" I said out loud with as much bubbliness as I could muster. My toddler babble, by this time, was becoming quite understandable."

"Hush, Josie," came a stern warning from Dad.

"I wasn't expecting that response from him at all. I shrank a little bit because I thought I did something wrong, I just didn't know what that was. I put my head down on Dad's shoulder and studied the new little sister I was being forced to accept. Whatever was she staring at? She had looked at each of us, and seemed to estimate our value or function; then she stared at the place on the porch where the boys were standing before they ran off into the backyard. I looked over there too. I searched all over to see if I could find what was so interesting. There were the chairs on the porch with the big stripes in the upholstery and the white wicker table. Surely, those things were not what kept her gaze. I looked at the enormous potted plant with the huge leaves that shined in the sunlight but I couldn't see anything worth more than a glance. Maybe it was the giant bumblebee that was so fascinating for her; she was only a baby after all. She hadn't seen the big fat black and yellow insects before. But her gaze did not follow the flight pattern of the bee. She was studying that area where no one was standing just like she studied each one of us. It was kind of weird."

Chapter III: Jane

Now that you have heard the story of my arrival from my sister's point of view, I would like to relate the same events to you from my perspective. This is the day I met my family. Not only the wonderful parents and siblings who adopted me here on the physical plane but also those family members residing on the ethereal plane who would have the greatest impact in my life. I have done my best to recount the events as they occurred and to relay them to you with the same thought, feelings and observations I had then.

I feel I need to begin with the most basic of explanations of my entrance to the material plane because while everyone comes into this life in the same manner, not everyone comes into his or her family the same way. I should start at the beginning. I was conceived on Halloween night and am the result of a wild adolescent costumed party, too much alcohol, and the back seat of a station wagon in the parking lot of the local fast food restaurant. My birth mother, or rather I allow myself the conjecture that it was my birth mother's parents who decided that I should be adopted into a family that could care for me more appropriately than their teenaged daughter. The only unusual aspect of my prenatal development was that my birth was overdue by two full weeks. Unfortunately for my birth mother, I was conceived at a time when the 'best practice' in medicine was to let things happen at their own pace. I was placed with an agency months before my birth on the first Saturday in August, and as a planned adoption, I was presented to my new family at the age of 6 days. By my reckoning, that means I was conceived on Halloween night and given to my new family on Friday the 13th. I have often wondered if the Universe was trying to tell me something. Mine was not an auspicious beginning.

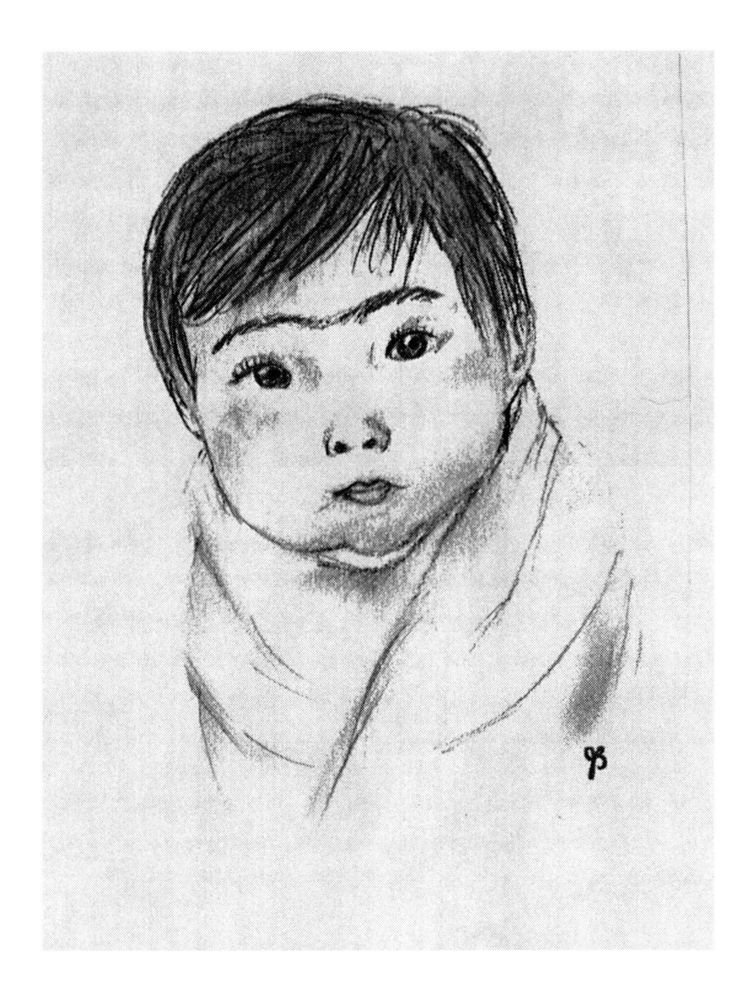

BABY JANE

When I arrived at what was to be my childhood residence, no one was there. The older woman who worked for the adoption agency was clearly a bit miffed at the lack of response when she knocked on the door, but told me in a calm but crackly voice, "Not to worry child, we will simply wait for them to return. I am certain your family won't be too long, they knew you were arriving today and I am confident they would not want to keep me…err, you waiting." I didn't see that I had any sort of real choice in the matter, so I didn't complain about it. Then on the side porch of what I had been told would be my new home, I saw this beautiful, swirling, purple mist with many beams of light of different colors and widths. It was really quite lovely. I would have liked to enjoy it longer but it disappeared as quickly as it had appeared and where it had been stood an odd looking group of people. I admit my experience with fashion was quite limited to what I had seen in the six days I had been alive, but none of these people were dressed like anyone I had seen before. There was what I now know to be an Early American settler, a teacher from the American West, a marine from the First World War and a 1920s "flapper". I was very interested in them, and they seemed to be really quite interested in me. They stayed on the porch and spoke to each other, but none of them talked to the adoption agency social worker or to me. The agency lady did not acknowledge their presence either. I looked from the group back to the social worker and back to the group. Don't they like her? I guess she does seem sort of standoffish. Maybe she scares them a little bit? I know she scares me. I listened to their conversation.

The American West woman said, "I wonder what is holding up Gillius and Lucille? There cannot possibly be anything more important to them than to welcome a rebirth to the material plane!"

The flapper laughed. "Oh, Caroline, you know that Gillius does as Gillius chooses. I would imagine that Lucille is quite fit to be tied with him right about now."

The early American settler added, "'Tis true. 'Tis not in Gillius' nature to move in a hurried manner; Patience is our best course this moment."

The Marine said, "I have no worry about Gillius arriving. I am certain Lucille will be sure he does so. I do wonder why that old sweat Levi has not yet shown himself. I would think he would want to be the first on scene to greet Madeline."

"Oh, Mel, honey, you are so out of it sometimes!" The flapper was incredulous. "Levi will be without Madeline now. You know they are cut from the same bolt of cloth. They had spent their last material lifetime together and even came over to our side together. Now he has to think about his life on the ethereal plane without her. Even though he can watch her, not talking to her is going to be really rough on him."

Madeline? I thought; who is Madeline? Suddenly, I heard the sounds of crunching and cracking. The old woman had been standing by her automobile carrying me face forward instead of over her shoulder. When she turned toward the noises I got a full view of what was coming our way. It was a dusty car pulling a large plastic looking trailer over the stone driveway. There were a lot of people inside the car. I guessed that they had been on a long trip to somewhere very dry and sandy. They certainly did make a lot of noise. Then I heard the old woman say, "Well finally! You see, child, I was right when I told you they would not keep me…I mean you waiting very long. I am certain your new family members are all very excited to meet you."

There was a flurry of activity as people jumped out of the car and quickly came over to where the woman was standing there holding me. There was a man carrying a little girl, another bigger girl, two boys and woman who it seemed could not wait to grab a hold of me. When the old woman handed me over she said, "Don't concern yourselves, we haven't been waiting too terribly long. I did think you would have been home to meet your new daughter though, Mrs. La Roi."

"Aha!" I thought, "She said daughter; so this is my mother and my last name is La Roi. I like it." I looked at my mother. She had kind eyes. I liked that too. My first impression of my mother was that she seemed nice enough. At least Mother appeared to be much friendlier than this old adoption agency lady. She smelled better too. I took that as a good sign.

"Oh my, Miss Peachtree, I am so very, very sorry to have kept you waiting! We had a little bit of unexpected car trouble on the way home." My new mother was visibly mortified at their delay.

"Well," the old woman said, "if you had expected the car trouble, then I would suppose your husband would have taken steps to avert it, wouldn't he?"

My mother looked at her for a moment clearly uncertain of how to respond, but then turned back to me and made these funny sounds. Oooh! Cooo! Cutchey Coo. I did not understand what she was saying at all. I wondered what language she was speaking. I was looking forward to learning it. It sounded like it might be fun!

"Now, I will need a name for the birth certificate and the adoption forms to be filed with the Courthouse," the social worker crackled as she pulled papers out of her bag. "I would like to get this paperwork filed today. I hadn't expected to be delayed waiting for your arrival but I can still make it in time if we are able to hurry through these documents."

Suddenly, there was more movement on the porch. The purple haze with beaming lights was back and, at the same time, the two boys who had shown brief interest in me ran away to somewhere behind the brick house. I looked from the porch to the boys who moved so quickly and then back to the porch; in place of the pretty lights and purple haze there now stood two more oddly dressed people. One was an older woman with a beautiful cane, a lovely hat, and a high collared dress. The other was a sort of middle-aged roundish man wearing what looked like one of the bed sheets I had seen in the hospital where I was born.

It seemed as if the others who got there earlier were waiting for them before coming over to our little gathering. The new arrivals moved into the area where the boys had earlier been craning to see what I looked like. I watched them with great curiosity. No one else of the remaining group, not mother, or father, or either of the two girls acknowledged any of the new people who stepped forward. I remember I found that interesting. The few people I had encountered during my limited life usually at least greeted one another when their paths crossed.

"Has her name yet been given?" asked the man in the sheet.

"Shh! We are just about to find out," said the American west woman.

Father spoke first. "We have given this a lot of thought and decided to call her Julia." I remember thinking, "Julia, Julia La Roi. Wow, that's a pretty name. I really like it." But, then Mother followed up with, "I don't know Charles. She doesn't really look like a Julia. Does she?" Mother studied me intently as Father shook his head slightly.

"No, dear," he said, "I don't believe she does look like a Julia. But then I am not certain what a Julia should look like either. What name do you think fits her?"

I was a bit disappointed. "I don't look like a Julia? I wonder what I do look like." I thought to myself while the conversation continued.

The Victorian lady said apparently to my new parents, "Julia is a fine name, you should stay with it."

Unfortunately, they didn't seem to hear her or they chose to ignore her because my mother then stated with absolute certainty, "Her name is Jane!"

"Alright, dear," said my father, "If you are happy with Jane, then Jane it is."

My father then leaned over a bit so the girl in his arms could get a better look at me and said, "Look, Josie, this is your new baby sister. Her name is Jane."

Our mother then addressed the older girl, "Joaney, please get the boys and start unpacking the camper and car."

Joaney whined. "Why do I always have to get the boys?" As she stomped off to the back of the house I heard her yell, "James! Alvin! Mom says you have to unload the car and camper *right now!"*

So, I thought, "My sisters' names are Josie and Joaney and I get Jane? I liked Julia better. Since the other little girl seems to think I look funny, maybe that has something to do with it."

Then from the group of oddly dressed people, I heard the American West woman in the long cotton skirt say, "Oh dear, Jane is such a plain and uninspiring name. Lucille, you and Gillius are the strongest ones here, can't you try to convince Pauline to go back to Julia?"

"So", I thought, "my mother's name is Pauline and father's name is Charles."

It seemed that Lucille was the lady in high-collared dress. I looked at her pleadingly. I was truly hoping she might speak to Mother and convince her that Julia was a much better choice. But then I heard from the man wearing a marine uniform.

"Look! Everyone! Look at Jane! I'm sure she sees us!"

"Oh, don't be ridiculous Melvin!" said the Victorian lady. "You know as well as we all do that once we are reborn to the material plane, the veil of all existence lowers and we lose the ability to see or interact with the energy of any one on the ethereal plane."

"You might wish to reconsider that, Lucille," said the man in the sheet. "Her eyes just met mine as I began speaking. I believe Jane can both see and hear us!"

The early American settler stepped forward and I shifted my gaze to focus on him. "I assert both Melvin and Gillius are correct in their statements, Lucille. The little one *can* see and hear us!"

The woman with the American West clothing said, "Well, Jane is clearly your name now, young miss." I looked over toward her and she continued, "And yes, Lucille, she definitely knows we are here."

The flapper chimed in as my eyes met hers. "I agree! The little darling definitely knows we're here, don't you, precious?"

I smiled and kicked my feet at her. She looked really sparkly and I liked the feather on her headband. She smiled a lot too.

The lady called Lucille said, "Goodness, I believe you are all absolutely correct." Then, she addressed me directly. "Jane, can you see me? Can you hear me?"

I looked right at her, and smiled. "Of course, I can see you and hear you," I thought. "What a silly thing to ask."

"Oh, it is not quite as silly as you think, my dear!" said Lucille.

"You heard what I was thinking?"

"Yes, Jane, I heard what you were thinking. Did anyone else hear Jane as well?" Lucille inquired of her group.

"I did," said the early American.

"I did too," said the American west lady.

"I heard you precious!" said the sparkly lady.

The man in the sheet shook his head "no".

Melvin the marine spoke next. "I didn't hear a thing. Why are you, Jacob and Caroline and Louise able to hear her but Gillius and I are not?"

Lucille spoke again. "I do not know the answer to that question. This is uncharted territory for all of us. I think for right now the best thing for us to do is to retreat to the council chambers on the ethereal plane and discuss this miracle."

The others seemed to agree with her as they smiled brightly at me and waved their goodbyes.

"Until we meet again, precious!" the sparkly lady called to me as she blew me a kiss.

They stepped back a bit and the purple haze appeared to engulf them like a fog rolling in. They were gone and I was left with mother, father, and Josie, who stuck her tongue out at me. Clearly, she was not thrilled that I joined her family.

Chapter IV: The Council

After our first encounter in the front yard of my home, the six members of the family council who had greeted me that day returned to the ethereal plane and held an emergency meeting. I have been told this story over and over again by each member of the council, so much so that I feel as if I were actually there when it happened. It was, after all, supposed to be a simple observational visit of a family member's rebirth to the material plane. As it turned out quite differently, I guess I really rocked their world. They have described themselves as being so very excited and nervous and even anxious over their ability to communicate with me. They also had a great deal of trepidation regarding the implications of that ability. I have put together a composite narrative of that council meeting from the many times it was recounted to me.

Together, the family Council quietly traversed the vortex-like tunnel created by the purple haze. Each was lost in thought as they stepped back into the seemingly limitless empty space that is the ethereal plane.

"Whose turn is it to create the council room?" asked Louise who was now holding a drink in her hand.

Lucille tapped her cane on the floor with significantly more force than she had when she opened the misty portal for Gillius and herself. This time the tapping of her cane brought forth a sudden and powerful flash of lights and the booming sound of tremendous rolling thunder. In front of them, where nothng had been before was now a great room, with a huge Victorian era wooden table. A judge's gavel was neatly placed at the seat considered to be the 'head' position. There were seven chairs around the table, but only 6 members were present.

"Wait, Lucille!" exclaimed Jacob. "'Twas my opportunity to create the council room!"

"Don't be a whining child, Jacob," said Caroline. "Clearly there are more important things to worry about right now!"

"Everyone, take your seat!" ordered Gillius. "This emergency meeting of the Quintus family council is convened." With that proclamation, he banged the gavel and all members present sat down. Gillius occupied the head of the table and Lucille sat opposite him in the other end seat as if to signify that these two spirits were the family elders. Gillius made a small gesture with his hand that changed the judge's gavel into a beautiful round marbled stone and the wooden base into one made of matching marble.

There was a single empty chair at the end of the table adjacent to Lucille. "And where is Levi?" an obviously irritated Lucille inquired. "I know he was upset that Madeline, now Jane, left our plane and I know he misses her deeply but we have called everyone to Council. He should be here."

If I might be allowed to interrupt the story for just a brief moment, I need to provide a bit of background information. Levi is my Uncle. He was my mother's brother in his last lifetime on the material plane and he raised me during my previous existence there after my parents were killed in an industrial accident. He took me in when I was very young and did his best to teach me everything he knew. Levi was a professor of physics when the field was rapidly changing to develop nuclear capabilities. As a single man, taking on a small girl must have been quite a shock to his system. He did not have a great deal of money but he did not let that get in the way and treated me as lovingly as any father ever could. He did the most important thing of all. He gave me his time and his attention. Levi was everything to me; he was my whole world. So when I was in my late twenties and he announced he was going to England to work on a project for the government during the Second World War, there was absolutely no question that I would accompany him. And, since he had taught me everything he knew, we really worked well together. But I need to get back to telling you of the emergency council meeting. To recount, everyone was there in the council chamber, except for Uncle Levi. He hadn't shown up to the visit with my new family either and Lucille was quite frankly annoyed.

After her proclamation that Levi's presence was necessary, all members held hands and closed their eyes, it was Louise who spoke. "We combine our energy and send a call to Council to Levi. We require your presence immediately."

A swirling, purple mist appeared in the doorway of the room. It created a seemingly endless corridor or tunnel. A tall man in a tweed coat and hat, wearing a vest walked casually along the corridor toward them. He was smoking a pipe and was trailed by a wide emerald green beam of light. When he reached the opening at the end he fully materialized or rather as energy only, 'etherealized' into the Council room.

"And what is so important that you summon me to Council?" said Levi, who looked like a professor and spoke with a heavy Dutch accent.

"A miracle has taken place, Levi," said Lucille as she clasped her hands together in excitement. "You know our Madeline, who incidentally is now called Jane, has been reborn. The veil of all existence has been lifted and she can see and hear us; and we her."

"My," said Levi as he thoughtfully puffed on his pipe. "That is quite an unexpected turn of events isn't it? I wonder what the Universal Energy has planned for...Jane, is it? It must be an interesting life for her indeed. And how does this affect us? Should we interact with her? My mind is suddenly flooded with questions. If the veil has been lifted, does she remember us and her life here?"

Again, to interrupt just briefly: I feel I have to say that Levi has always impressed me with his ability to take apart or break down any problem. This gift is not limited to his physics and mathematical prowess but to the human psyche as well. I have often thought if he had not chosen the field of nuclear physics as his profession that he would have been equally suited to psychiatry as well. But I must take you back to the Council meeting; Caroline, who was a teacher and last lived during the time of expansion into the American West, was more of a take-no-prisoners kind of woman. If she knew she were right then she attacked any problem without hesitation, but if she had any question in her mind of safety, especially where children were concerned, then caution was her path. When she lived on the material plane, her life was physically and emotionally hard. She had to be determined and resolute about any decisions she made as any one of them could mean life or death. So I understand why her initial gut feeling was to hold back.

Caroline interjected. "Of course we cannot interact with her until she returns to the ethereal plane. Anything we might say or do could radically alter the family path. Recta electio, recta ratio in omni tempore. Our family motto: The Right Choice for the Right Reason Every Time," she said as she pointed to the family coat of arms on the wall above Gillius' head. "This is the standard you have set for us, Gillius, and these are the words we all live by. I think caution is the best course of action."

"But we always watch the material plane," said Melvin, "and we try to guide our family members there. And I'll just say it: I like to be the voice of conscience, to whisper in the ear of someone trying to make a decision. 'Specially those decisions that affect not only them but any one of us who could be reborn at any time and have to deal with the fallout of their choices. I say we should get our licks in while we can."

Now, I have to admit Melvin is one of my family favorites. He maintained that easy southern manner after he crossed over. He speaks with a drawl common in the Tennessee mountains where he last lived and still wears his World War I Marine Corps uniform as proudly as the day he died in it.

Melvin continued. "C'mon, Caroline! How often have you reached out through the dreams of someone you were watchin' to give them a little push down the right path? The strongest of us have even physically moved objects to remind our loved ones of something or to help them find their way through uncertain times. You remember, Lucille, like when you made the pennies fall off the night stand to remind your great, great grandson to think of his grandmother who always gave him a penny when she saw him. When he thought of her, he thought of what she would do in his situation and he made the right choice and followed through with it. I think the question is that if we watch Madel...I mean Jane, and she see us, will that cause problems for either side? What is the safest tactical approach for all of us? Should we watch her through the view ports only?"

From what I have gathered from the different members of the Council who have told me this story, it was Louise who spoke next. Louise was a party girl from the roaring 20's. The vernacular would have been to call her a "flapper." I think that is a great way to describe her because Louise is just fun. Everything about her is fun. She seems to enjoy her ethereal life every bit as much as she did her physical one. According to Louise, "if you're not enjoying your life, you're not living." This credo was unfortunately the cause of her demise on October 29, 1929. If you remember your history classes, that day is also known as Black Tuesday. That was the day the stock market crashed and the roaring twenties came to an abrupt halt, as did the unfortunate stockbroker who landed directly on top of Louise after jumping out of a very high window. She was on her way into the speakeasy she ran to set up for the evening crowd, when she quite unexpectedly found herself on the ethereal plane. But in true Louise fashion, she chose to have fun with that too and brought the party with her.

Louise succinctly stated the dilemma by asking one question. "I don't like to think of us on different sides, Mel, honey. No matter which plane of existence we live on, we are all connected through family ties. Since Jane can see and hear us, and we can hear what she is thinking, then aren't we supposed to interact with her?"

"It is as yet unknown what it is the Universal Energy has planned for any of us, or for all of us as a family unit," interjected Jacob. "How is it that we should know the proper course of action for us to take now?"

I think Jacob is an interesting soul. He considers himself a second-generation early American settler but I see him as more of a frontiersman, although perhaps those two descriptors are not all that far apart. He is proper in his decorum but not unwilling to get his hands dirty by working hard and pitching in. There have been many times when I have enjoyed his tales of the actual happenings of life in early American history. There is no guile in Jacob. He is forthright and upright and holds fast to his ideals. I would not say that Jacob is easily swayed in his opinions, yet I would never consider him to be an unreasonable sort. Anyway, the meeting continued with everyone becoming quiet for a moment as if Jacob had given them all pause for thought.

"Hmmm." Gillius nodded as if pondering Jacob's statement.

Caroline spoke next. "We should watch from the ethereal plane and not cross to the material plane until we have a better understanding of what direction, if any, we should take."

"I agree with Caroline," said Lucille. "Keeping our distance may be the best course for all of us, Jane included."

"As do I," said Jacob. "'Tis surely the safest path."

"I'll jump on board too, I guess," a clearly disappointed Louise replied, "but I miss the little darling already."

"Alright then, a family council vote is in order," came Gillius' strong statesman voice. "All in favor of waiting and watching through view ports only until we have more information?"

Five ayes came from the members of the council. The two silent holdouts were Melvin and Levi.

"Opposed?" asked Gillius.

Two nays came from the opposite sides of the table from where Levi and Melvin were sitting.

Lucille said, "Alright, Levi, you know we work by unanimous vote, we have heard Melvin's objections already. What are your concerns?"

Levi stood and relit his pipe. "It occurs to me and will to you as well, when you all come to your senses from the excitement, that we must at least acknowledge the possibility, even likelihood, that Jane may be able to see and hear other energies besides ourselves. We do not know that it is only ours that she is aware of. What if she asks her human mother about people and conversations no one else can see or hear? A much more frightening possibility has also occurred to me. What if the Xu clan finds out about her ability and tries to use her for their own purposes?"

There was a collective gasp from the council members at the mention of the name Xu (shoo).

"They could misdirect her into doing their bidding and I do not even want to think about what horrible things could happen to her and to this family should Xu be able to join his family energy to ours. No one wants to admit that Zank Xu has launched a campaign to gather power on both the ethereal and material planes by connecting genetically and energetically with as many families as he can." Levi became angered and impassioned and pounded the table with his fist. "You all know to your souls that he is dangerous and probably evil even though he puts forth the face of sincerity. You just haven't admitted it to each other. Well, I am saying it out loud. He is dangerous and Jane is in trouble, as are we, if no one is there to guide her or to help her avoid him."

"Oh my goodness! You are right, Levi," a suddenly frightened Caroline said. "What ever shall we do?"

"Yes, your thoughts are clear as always and you have spoken well, Levi," said Lucille. "Steps must be taken to watch over Jane on the material plane. She must be protected!"

"How do we do that?" asked Louise. "We could send someone who can understand her thoughts, but that leaves Melvin and Gillius out. How do we choose which of us should go to the material plane and how do we decide how long he or she should stay?"

"Should we not come and go as we are needed?" asked Jacob. "We could alternate our presence and stand guard over her, each one of us in turn."

"No, I will go," stated Levi firmly but calmly. "I am the one she has had the most recent life experience with; that may be of some help and be less frightening for her."

"We don't even know if she will be able to see and hear you or you her, since you missed the family gathering to greet her," said Lucille in an accusatory tone.

"Well then," replied Levi in the same firm but even tone, "there truly is only one way to find out, isn't there? I will go immediately."

Levi closed his eyes for a brief moment and the purple mist formed just behind him. He stood, tipped his hat to the other Council members, stepped through the mist and disappeared from the room.

Chapter V: Uncle Levi

This is one of my favorite memories. It's simple and short but decidedly a happy moment for me. I want to tell you about the first time I met Uncle Levi. The first time during this life, that is.

I had been put to bed for the night, but as a nine month old, I could sit up, and look around the confines of my room if I wanted too. Mother kept my sisters and brothers and me on a really tight schedule. It seemed to me like every moment of my day was planned so at night I would sit up and look around and think until I finally fell asleep. We went to church every Sunday and I would listen to the preacher talk to the congregation. One of his sermons said that there is a time for everything. It was from Ecclesiastes. He said, "There is a time for everything and a season for every activity under heaven." I have often thought that Mother may have taken that sermon far too literally. She designated what time I should awaken, eat, have my diaper changed, burp, and bathe, change clothing and play. I was really tired of the tedium of it already.

At this particular moment, I was bored out of my mind and was searching around the room for something interesting to focus on. I kept looking for the purple haze with the bright and colorful beams of light to return, but I hadn't seen it anywhere since the first day I came to my new home. I couldn't imagine why the people I had seen that day hadn't come back. They seemed really interested in me when we met. I had recently decided that maybe I had gotten that wrong and they really were not all that concerned about me but I couldn't help it, I still hoped to see the pretty purple mist and colorful lights again. And then, just as I sat there wishing for it, the haze appeared a few feet in front of my crib.

Mother had left the room only moments earlier, when a tall man wearing a tweed coat with graying hair and a pipe clenched in his teeth calmly stepped through the haze and was trailed by beautiful dark green lights. He smiled and approached the side of my crib. He looked at me with the same curiosity I had for him. It took a few moments but he finally asked a question. He spoke with what I now know to be a heavy Dutch accent.

UNCLE LEVI

"So, Jane, now is it? Well, I suppose I will have to get used to it, and so will you. Hello, there little lady. I am your Uncle Levi and I will be taking care of you from what people here would call 'the other side'. Oh, your momma and poppa will look after your physical needs. They love you and will feed you and give you clothes and toys." He looked around a bit as he continued. "They have provided this lovely house for you to live in. I cannot replace them and have no wish to do so. I am here to give you advice and offer counsel when you need it. I represent the rest of your family, some of whom you met earlier. Don't you worry, little Miss Jane; you are extraordinary, so much so that it seems you have been granted access to your entire family from all generations and walks of life. We will all do our best to take exceedingly excellent care of you."

"I have more family?" I thought.

"Oh, my dear, you most certainly do!" He said. "You have family one hundred generations old and we all stand ready and willing to help guide you!"

"He heard me!" I thought with surprise and clapped my hands with glee.

He smiled and nodded at me, let out a puff of smoke from his pipe and calmly walked back into a purple misty haze.

I still remember how happy I was to meet Uncle Levi. I did not know why at the time, but he seemed so comforting or maybe comfortable would be a better choice of words. At that moment, everything was right in my tiny little world. I have learned what followed from other Council members.

Levi stepped back into the council room where everyone was still in their seats discussing the situation just as they had been when he left.

"Jane is nine months old now and seems to be doing well", he said with some pride in his voice.

"Alright, Levi," said Gillius approvingly. "You have the strongest connection to her since you raised Jane in her last incarnation and you two left the material plane together during that bombing in the Second World War. I propose that you personally watch over our Jane, teach her as you did before, and call upon the family for support when we are needed."

"That is a reasonable solution," offered Lucille. "Until we have more information and understanding of the ramifications of our interaction with Jane, it is better to limit her direct exposure to us to a single family member." The other members of the council nodded their approval and Gillius banged the marble stone onto its base to signal the meeting had come to an end. The room dissolved into a mist and the council members each disappeared with their own flash of light each of a different color.

Chapter VI: James And Alvin

I realize I have been focusing on the family members on the ethereal plane. It is about time I introduced you to some more of those I lived with at home. You have already met Josie so now I'll introduce my brothers, James and Alvin. Grandmother would say, "Those boys are peas in a pod." I can best explain her assessment by relating to you moments I myself witnessed while coalescing some information provided to me by James of the day they first met each other.

It was another beautifully warm and sunny day at the La Roi home. "James!" Mother said loudly, "Make sure you and Alvin clean your plates and throw away everything you use when you are done!"

"Sure, okay, Ma," James yelled back.

We were having what our parents called a family get-together at our house. That meant that the whole family, all the aunts and uncles and, best of all, cousins, came from across the fields and across the road to eat and play and spend some time together. These were fun days. Full of volleyball and badminton, yard darts, horseshoes and croquet. The games were all friendly of course. This was all possible because our whole family lived on the same road. You see, our mother's father was a farmer. Grandpa and Grandma were really smart and very practical business people as well. They gave each of their own children two acres of land. One acre on which to build a home and an additional acre to garden and grow produce for the grandchildren who certainly would come. Grandma and Grandpa knew that having their own children's families in close proximity would ensure there would always be a grandchild around to do their bidding. Fortunately, it also meant there was always a cousin or two around to play with when wanted. These 'get-together' days usually took place on a Saturday or Sunday, whichever day Grandma chose.

Marie (Aunt Annie and Uncle Hank's oldest) and James were standing in the backyard under the giant cottonwood tree waiting for their turn to get hotdogs, when she asked James, "Why don't you play with Jane like you do with Josie?"

"Jane is younger and besides, she's just weird. She isn't fun like Josie and she sure isn't cute," James said.

Marie, whose coal black curly hair and great big dimples made her a family favorite, said, "You're just being mean James! You think just because you're a boy you get to do and say whatever you want! You are supposed to be nice to your little sister and make her feel like a princess no matter what she looks like. A big brother's job is to protect his little sister's feelings, always. That is what you are *supposed* to do! I'm glad you're not my brother!"

"Yeah, well so am I!" said James. "Hey, wait a minute," he continued his protest, "I play with Josie and I sometimes watch her when Mom tells me too, but Jane is just weird! She watches me all the time. I can feel her eyes on me. It's like I'm her science experiment. She kind of freaks me out. All she does is watch. She doesn't talk, doesn't even make baby noises. She doesn't ever cry like a normal baby does. Look, I don't know what it is, but there is something really wrong with her!"

I have to admit, what he said really hurt my feelings. But Marie came to the rescue.

"You are the meanest brother ever James La Roi!" exclaimed Marie. "No wonder Jane doesn't try to talk to you; I wouldn't either if I were her. Big meany!"

Marie stomped off to tell Aunt Annie what horrible things James had said. James got hotdogs for Alvin and himself and went over to where Alvin was piling up the potato salad, baked beans, chips and punch. They had really loaded up their plates and then carefully walked over to sit under the weeping willow in front of the swing set Dad had made for us.

It was really more of a gym set than a swing set. There were swings of course, but we had climbing bars, and a cool teeter-totter, and a slide too. Dad was really great at making things.

They started stuffing their faces just as soon as they sat down. Those boys could really eat. After James had inhaled one of his hotdogs he thought maybe he should ask Alvin about me. "Alvin," he said, "do you think Jane is weird?"

Alvin was our big brother, even though James had been adopted first. Mom and Dad got James when he was six months old. The story goes that one day, when James was four, he came downstairs from a nap and found this five-year-old strange looking boy with bright blonde hair and really big ears playing with his toys. James can still remember it like it just happened.

"Who are you? Those are *my toys!*" James yelled as loud as he could, hoping our mother would come running in to save his stuff. He burst into tears. Alvin just looked up at him and smiled a great big wide smile. James said he thought he could see all of Alvin's teeth.

But Alvin was not deterred by the tears of a four year old. He said, "Hi! I'm Alvin and I am your new brother so these are my toys too. You *do* know how to share, don't you?"

Alvin originally came from Kentucky so he had a sort of a twang to his speech. His family had moved north in search of work at the many automobile factories in the Detroit area. I never did know exactly what happened, but Alvin and his brothers and sisters were placed in foster care. Each went to a different home. We were lucky to get Alvin; I don't know why any of the other families he stayed with didn't choose to adopt him. I have heard he was a bit of a troublemaker and I can believe it. I would still describe him as mischievous. To our parents' credit, they believe there is always room for one more and were undaunted by his previous exploits. I'm sure glad they kept him and made him part of our family.

"No," James said, "what's that?" All the while he was sniffling and wiping his face to dry it. He was being truthful. He really didn't know what sharing meant. The only other child in the house at the time was my sister Joaney. She is four years older than James and she was a real "girly"' girl. They didn't have any toys in common. James didn't play with her dolls and she never wanted to play with his trucks or Lincoln Logs so sharing was never required learning until Alvin arrived.

"Well," said Alvin, "sharing is when you let someone else play with your stuff and might even play along with them. Don't worry, it's okay you don't know how. I've been in lots of other houses with lots of other kids since I got put in foster care. I'm really good at sharing. I'll show you."

There was something about Alvin that immediately put everyone at ease. James sat down on the floor across from him and they built a fort with the Lincoln Logs together and then ran trucks through the fort making engine noises and dumping cargo. They had a really fun time. It was the first of many. They have been brothers and best friends ever since. That's why I knew that Alvin would find a way to make all the mean things James had said okay.

"Everybody is weird somehow," said Alvin while chewing a big spoon of potato salad. "Jane just doesn't know how to hide it yet. Don't worry, she'll figure it out sooner or later."

"So you like her?" James asked.

"Sure," said Alvin. "She's quiet and she don't fuss or demand attention like Josie does. She doesn't bother me at all. Yep, I like her just fine. She is almost the perfect little sister."

"What do you mean, almost?" James inquired.

"Well," Alvin began slowly, "there is that eyebrow thing she's got. It does kind of make her look funny, sort of like my ears do me. When she starts school her feelings are going to get hurt a lot by other kids. Until she learns to blow those other kids off, you and me are going to have to kick some butt for her. That's okay, though, I like kicking butt!"

"Oh," James said, "I hadn't thought of that. Is that what big brothers do? Beat up other kids who pick on our little sisters? Is that what Marie meant by protecting her?"

"Oh hell yea!" said Alvin with great enthusiasm. "That's one of the few perks of the job! Look, James, little sisters are a huge pain in the butt most of the time, that's their job. Our job is to make sure no one else tortures them, other than us, of course."

By the time they finished their hot dogs and potato chips, James had decided that I was okay and that he would protect me and be as nice to me as he could be. Alvin was right. I was going to have a hard time with other kids and I was going to need them. James felt pretty good about that and, honestly, so did I.

Chapter VII: Sibling Rivalry

I liked my brothers a lot when we were growing up. They seemed to have fun no matter what they were doing. My sister Joaney, on the other hand, seemed to have less enjoyment out of daily life. I don't know if it was just her personality or the issues of an adolescent girl, but Joaney did not really seem to like much of anything. My brothers always found a way to make Joaney funny at least to me. Now that I think about it, maybe that's why she always seemed so put upon. James and Alvin were a handful at best, not that anything they did was ever mean or spiteful, but Joaney was always more of a princess and the rest of us were her commoners. I don't think she liked it when the commoners ran amok. I'll tell you about one of the earliest episodes I can remember. It still makes me laugh to this day.

Mother and Father had gone out for the evening and Joaney was supposed to be babysitting the rest of us. I don't think her method of childcare is one that Mother would particularly approve of but it is what she usually did when she was "stuck" with us, as she would say. It seemed to me that practicing make-up application was really her true calling in life.

She was smart but didn't really succeed at school. Joaney was in her room applying her false eyelashes (for what seemed like the thousandth time) while the curling iron heated up on the dresser next to the makeup table with the really big mirror. There was a smaller independent magnifying mirror strategically placed in front of her so she could be certain the glue line of the fake lashes did not show. Josie had gotten hold of her blush brush and managed to apply the remnants of the powder to her cheeks. There was way too much blush powder on the brush and Josie looked like she had painted big red lines of war paint on each side of her face.

I was sitting on the floor intently watching the show my sisters were putting on as each was fascinated with the decoration of her face. I heard some quiet rustling and giggling outside the door but my sisters were too busy making themselves look beautiful (or so they thought) to notice. Joaney was adjusting the left eyelash for what seemed like the 100th time when the door silently opened and the boys snuck in. Alvin came in first. He was wearing a gorilla mask and softly crawled in on all fours so he wouldn't be seen in the mirrors. James was right behind him. He crawled too. They quietly crept right up to Joaney's left side. Alvin very slowly began raise up from the crawling position to a crouch so his masked face was just about between Joaney's elbow and shoulder. He just stayed there staring at her without moving a muscle. It seemed like he hovered there a long time but I suppose it was the anticipation of what was about to happen that made it seem longer. It was really less than a minute. Josie who had moved onto the right side was reaching for another make-up brush. Joaney was just about to admonish her when James, snickered a bit. Just as Joaney looked to her left with her false eyelash still dangling half off of her lid, Alvin and his mask popped up just enough to be right at her line of sight.

"Boo!" said Alvin.

Joaney screamed and screamed. There was a horrified contorted look on her face. Her eyes got so big; I thought they would pop out. Her mouth was open so wide I could see her tonsils. Her arms were flailing wildly and the big box of powder she would brush on after she put on the liquid called foundation flew just over my head and hit the closet door. The lid had not been secured so the powder erupted into the air. I was covered with it. My hair, my clothes, and my legs were all coated with the beige dust. I coughed and rubbed my eyes. Joaney was still screaming. I thought her voice was stuck and maybe she couldn't stop. She knocked over her chair and Alvin trying to get out of the room. The boys laughed hysterically! They were literally unable to get up off of the floor they were laughing so hard. Josie, who had also been taken by surprise shrieked once, but then saw Joaney's overreaction and started laughing uncontrollably as well. I have to admit, even though I was coughing and sneezing, it really was pretty funny.

To my oldest sister, dating was a career move. She'd had a steady boyfriend but he broke up with her months before this incident. She went through this phase of staying in her room and not coming out except for school and meals. Mother called it depression. I was tired of hearing about it. I didn't understand a lot of the interactions between people as it was, but long, drawn-out emotional problems seemed silly to me. I had heard Grandma say, "Listen, Joaney, if you don't love yourself no one else will either. If that boy isn't the right one, let him go. God will send the right man at the right time. In the mean time, it's your job to make yourself the best person you can be." I thought that sounded like pretty good advice, but I was going to have to wait several years to be old enough to worry about it.

Joaney finally did pull herself out of her depression with some prodding and poking from Mother, Father and our two brothers. She was back to acting like the family 'princess' when she met this guy named Gary. He wore a letterman jacket everywhere. I think Joaney really liked it because it seemed like she wanted him to give it to her. He also wore sunglasses everywhere, even inside. I guess he thought he looked cool with them on, I know Joaney sure thought he did.

"Oooh, G-a-r-y!" Alvin would draw the name out using a mock girl's voice so he could tease our sister.

"You are soooo handsome and soooo sweet!" James would mimick Alvin in the same sort of girlish voice. Then they would turn around and cross their arms so they could pat or rub their backs. It looked like someone was hugging them. Of course, all of this was accompanied by loud kissing noises.

Joaney really hated when they did that sort of thing. She would get angry and yell to anyone who was within earshot, "Why couldn't I be an only child!" She would storm away and slam the nearest door for dramatic effect. This was a fairly regular event in the La Roi house.

I don't know if she liked any of her siblings, but I heard her tell Mother that I in particular was just "too much". I wondered what that meant.

Section II: The Story Begins

Life on the ethereal plane manifests as the energy living it either intends it to be or accepts it to be. Most, although not all, inhabitants recreate some version of the life they lead in the physical world when they last lived there. I've been told it's comfortable for them. Some, however, create their idyllic environment, an after-lifestyle (as I like to call it) at the expense of others.

A lot can happen in a very short period of time on both planes of existence. I was not yet two years old when things heated up in the ethereal realm. The time has come for me to tell you about the only soul I have ever heard any one of my ancestors speak of with anything other than kind words. You may remember that Uncle Levi mentioned someone named Xu in his earlier discussions with the Council. I need to tell you about him now.

Zank Xu is a very scary character. He is without a doubt the greatest nemesis my family ever faced. Thinking about him sends shivers up my spine even now. He is, of course, one of the reasons I have chosen to write the story put forth upon these pages. There must be some historical documentation, even if it is in story form only, of what has happened so that future generations may learn and understand.

I have done my best to condense the many descriptions and tales of him into a single encompassing chronicle.

Chapter VIII: Zank Xu

Zank Xu (Zank Shoo) was tall, thin and arrogant. His long shiny raven black hair had just the tiniest touch of grey at the temples. His broad forehead accentuated his high prominent cheekbones and black deep-set eyes. He wore a meticulously groomed goatee that he kept braided and waxed to hide what he considered to be a less than strong chin.

He was intensely domineering and craved power and control and would stop at nothing to get it. Zank Xu was certain he was destined for extraordinary greatness and expected complete success at every turn.

On the ethereal plane, he created for himself an opulent palace of imperial status. It was more than he had on the physical world but no less than he was certain he deserved. His family members were his servants during physical life and he made sure they remained so during their spiritual energy existence.

He would control both the material and the ethereal planes. It was his duty, it was his right and he would find a way to make it so. Zank Xu would pontificate to his uneasy trio of advisors (as he called them) and they have represented his exact words as follows:

"I have long searched for a way to determine which of my family members will be reborn to the material plane. If I can find a way to communicate with them after rebirth, I can use their physical form to carry out my wishes there and gain control of my family assets and functions in that realm."

ZANK XU

Zank Xu's last life on the material plane came during the Later Jin Dynasty in 12th century China. He was the only son born into an extremely wealthy family and was treated with great deference and respect. His family refused to dress or wear their hair in the custom of the time. They set their own standard and expected everyone else including the Governor of the province to admire their choice but forbade them from emulation. He was taught to believe he was special. His family was important, which made him the only heir even more special. Oh yes, Zank Xu was very, very special, of that he was absolutely certain.

He was provided an excellent education in his youth. His father had taught him to create wealth and to run his business. The family business was trading in human traffic. He provided workers for landowners and soldiers for warlords. He provided this commodity by first trying to buy young people from their families. He would say to the father of a poor family, "I will give you ten pieces of gold for the services of your young son or daughter for three years. He or she will work in a field for a large landowner and will be provided with everything he or she needs. He or she will be given generous food, ample clothing and an excellent education. All he/she must do is work six hours each day and provide his/her best effort."

Of course, the young son or daughter would agree to go, some would even beg their father to allow them to go, so their family would be cared for; if the father would not consent to accept gold for his offspring then the father of Zank Xu would simply take the youngster at another time and place, and of course that child would never be heard from again.

Zank had developed his own philosophy of survival during his lifetime on the material plane and he carried it with him into his ethereal life.

"The weak and the needy will do anything and sell anything to survive, but from the strong, you must take what you want in a way that does not arouse suspicion. This is the way it is on both planes of existence. The more spiritual energy I can add to this family, the stronger I will become in both realms. I learned well at the knee of my father," Zank Xu would crow to his advisors. "Strange, though, I have not found his energy on either plane of existence. Hmm."

Now like you, hopefully, I found myself wondering how could anyone who had what seemed to be everything in life turn out to be so evil? Why would he have such a deep-seated need for power that it would continue to drive his reason for being even after physical death?

Well, it seems that the father of Zank Xu did not exactly teach his son everything about his business. While his father was alive, his family was all but treated as royalty and allowed to dress as they chose and to do as they wished just as long as proper remuneration for the privilege was offered to the Governor. I gather the Governor was a man not to be trifled with but neither was he a fool and he saw just how much money the father of Zank Xu could provide his coffers. He was willing to allow the family's behavior to continue just as long as the money was flowing his way. But as is the reality of all men, the father of Zank Xu died one day. This event left Zank in charge of the family business; with no idea of the monetary tribute he was to send to the Governor to maintain his family's lifestyle. Zank went on acting as if he were a person of the most supreme importance without paying the fare for nearly three years.

As you can imagine, this angered the Governor who sent an emissary to demand payment. When the Governor's emissary arrived, Zank was at dinner with his wife, mother and children. Not that he ate at the same table as they did, of course; he was too important for that. He took meals at a separate table with his eldest son. Their table sat on a platform in the dining area of the home so that he would always appear to be higher than everyone else in the room. The women and younger children ate at a smaller table and only after he was served first. A servant announced the arrival of the emissary and Zank flew into a rage at the disturbance of his meal by such an unworthy person. He made the emissary wait outside the door until he had finished and he took an extra helping of everything just to be certain the meal lasted as long as he could possibly make it. That way the emissary would know that he was far more important than the Governor and should be respected as such.

Finally, after he had finished the last drop of his tea, and paused to allow it to reach his stomach, Zank "graciously" granted the emissary an audience. The man stepped forward and flatly stated the Governor's demand for three years worth of payment and the next year's commitment in advance since he could no longer trust the Xu family to pay as required.

Zank Xu was furious! His anger swelled up in him to the point his eyes became darker than they already were.

"Does the Governor think me a fool? How utterly outlandish to say that my father paid him for the privilege of living as he saw fit! It is the Governor who should pay me, for it is I that allow him to maintain his lifestyle as he does. How dare he demand money from me! It is **I** that should demand payment from him!"

The emissary simply bowed as deeply as he could to show deference to Zank Xu and requested permission to return to the Governor with the answer provided him.

That was the biggest political mistake Zank Xu had ever made. He had allowed the emissary to return with his answer; an answer that so greatly angered the Governor he immediately dispatched an entire army to arrest the Xu family. They were taken by surprise in the very early hours of the morning. The Governor's men stormed into the house of Xu and arrested all of the family members including Xu's wife, mother, children and servants. They were left in the clothing they slept in and their hair in its unkempt state. They were tied together in a single line with the youngest child in front and Zank Xu at the rear and were marched, paraded really, in an effort to demean and demoralize them all the way to the Governor's mansion. All the while, the soldiers called attention to the Xus to anyone they encountered along the way so that the passersby might jeer or throw things at the family as they pleased.

The journey took weeks. They were not given any water or food and were not allowed to relieve themselves in private. It was only a matter of a very few days before the youngest child died from thirst and exhaustion and only a day after that before the next in line followed suit. By the time the group reached the home of the Governor, Zank Xu's mother and all of his children had died. His wife had lost her mind and was really quite unstable both mentally and physically. She had sung of the greatness of the Xu family as an act of defiance when the journey began, but now she sang the same song over and over and over as if it were a compulsion she could not restrain. Zank saw the devastation of his family but he could not comprehend its meaning. With the passing of each family member he felt an unfamiliar pain. Finally, one night as they were being held in the Governor's courtyard, he could contain that agony no longer and cried out to the sky.

"Why? Why is this happening to me? **I** am special. My family is special! What is the meaning of this torture?"

The Governor had stepped outside just in time to hear Xu's cries.

He responded, "The meaning of this torture, *you fool*, is to let you know that you are *not* special. *You* are nothing. *You* are as unimportant as this insect." With great drama, the Governor crushed a beetle under his boot for effect. "All you had to do was to send the same offering as your father did to maintain your lavish life, but you thought yourself too important, and now you have lost everything and everyone. I planned to keep your wife as payment for your lack of judgment but I now see that she is not worthy of my efforts. I had intended to lock you in a cage in the center square for all to see and humiliate for your foolishness, but now I realize that I can do better than that. I am confiscating all of your property, servants, and land. I will give you back your wife, such as she is (he looked down at Mrs. Xu with utter disdain) and leave you with the clothes on your backs. (The Governor actually spat these next words to them.) You are expelled from this province and will leave at once. If my men find you still in my jurisdiction within one month, you will be summarily executed. Now run, **you fool**!"

It took only a brief moment for Zank Xu to regain his wits after the Governor's pronouncement. He had been released from the tether that bound his family together during the forced march and in an odd moment of either love or pity he took a hold of his wife's frail hand. They ran as fast as they could muster and did not take even a moment to rest until they could no longer hear the Governor and his men laughing and calling after them.

Zank knew that there was no way with the vastness of the province that he and his wife would be able to reach its border by foot in the time allotted. Surely this was the Governor's plan. He intended to make sport of them and hunt them down like animals. Zank thought they might be safer if they hid up in the mountains. He felt certain there must be water there because the trees were green and plants were blossoming. He thought if they could get to the water supply, his wife's mind might return and she would come back to him.

Unfortunately, Mrs. Xu did not survive even after they reached the water. She was too far-gone both physically and mentally and she died in her husband's arms that same night. It was then as he buried his wife that an anguished and grief stricken Zank Xu made his eternal promise.

"Never!" He yelled to the sky. "Never again will I feel this powerless! Never again will I lose control! *Never!* I swear by my immortal soul I will regain my power; I will be as *supremely* important as I was and I *will* reform my family and lead them for all eternity! I **vow** it shall be so!"

Maybe I am just too much of a softy, but I have always found Zank Xu to be such a sad (but still evil) spirit. During the entirety of his childhood when his sense of self was being formed, he was taught that he was special. He believed it to be true since the information came from the people he trusted the most, his parents. But it was his father's need to continue the illusion of his own power, to maintain appearances for his son that eventually destroyed his son's family and in some ways his son. If only his father had been able to share with Zank the knowledge that he paid the Governor so his family could appear to be as important as they did, then Zank Xu might have been able to keep his family alive and may have turned out to be an altogether different sort of soul. It really is quite sad.

Chapter Ix: Louise And Melvin

Some of you may say that Zank Xu is to be pitied. If not for his father's deception, he might have continued to be selfish and arrogant, but probably would not have become evil. That's the trouble with supposing what might have been; we will really never know.

My family on the ethereal plane had their suspicions of the motives and plans of Zank Xu, but had no actual proof or direction to take to plan any sort of defense.

I mentioned earlier that Louise was a party girl and loved to have fun. She was also quite the businesswoman who provided a safe place of entertainment for any who might join her on the material plane and has chosen to continue that effort in her "afterlife;" and just as before, everyone was welcome. The first hint the family had of the pending trouble came from Louise's operation where well-lubricated enjoyment tends to allow information to flow freely.

The atmosphere was loud and boisterous at the speakeasy Louise created for herself. She sat in a booth at the center of the room along the back wall with many people bustling around and the music of the roaring '20s blaring in the background. She wore her favorite dress. It happened to be the one she was wearing the night she crossed over to the ethereal plane. It sparkled with thousands of sequins and had fringe along the hemline. It was sleeveless and too low cut for the time she lived in on the material plane. She wore a matching small headband with a huge contra-colored feather on the left side. She had a drink in her hand and music in her heart. This was where she was happiest and most comfortable on the material plane and so this was the home Louise created for herself in the ethereal realm.

The password of the day was to be given to the bouncer at the back ally entrance through a very small, eye-level sliding window in the door. Melvin arrived at Louise's and knocked on the door three times. The window slid aside quickly.

"Copasetic," said Melvin. The window slammed shut and the door opened.

Melvin walked in past the very large security man who opened the door and greeted the woman at the coat check desk.

"Hey, Tillie, looks like the joint is jumpin'."

Tillie smiled as she rearranged the hats on the shelf behind her. "Yep, it'll be a swell time tonight, Mel, but then it is every night at Louise's!" She laughed.

Melvin crossed the floor toward Louise, nodding and smiling at those patrons he recognized on the way.

"I love what you've done with the place!" he said as he approached Louise's table. "Cash or check?" he asked, inquiring whether he should kiss her now as a greeting or later as he said goodbye to leave the club.

"Ooh! Both!" said Louise as she stretched up a bit to meet his greeting. Melvin kissed her on the cheek and they both sat back into the booth.

"What do you think about our situation? I mean, of course about the veil of all existence being lifted in our little Jane. I may be beef-brained but I can't hold onto any sort of understanding. Why do you think it happened?" he asked.

"Well I know you are not beef-brained so what do you mean?" Louise asked as Mel ordered a drink from a waitress who had stopped by their table.

"I know we all believe that everything happens for a reason," Melvin continued, "but this one tickles my mind and shivers my spine at the same time. I am truly confounded and it sits really heavy in my thoughts. Tell me, Louise, you've got good insight, what do you think, really? Why has this happened in someone so small and with so little power to use it? Why was Jane given this gift? It's a gift that affects all of us. What are we supposed to do with it? "

"Well," said Louise swirling the ice cubes in her drink, "ever since Levi mentioned Zank Xu, I have specifically been watching his family's homes on the Asian continent through the view ports and as you well know most everyone who is anyone comes into this juice joint sooner or later. So, I have been paying special attention to certain people's chatter lately. I overheard a tête-à-tête between two members of the Xu clan right over there," Louise pointed to the adjacent table, "and I think I've put it together with what I have been watching the material plane."

An incredulous Melvin said, "Wait, the Xu clan comes here? I didn't think old Zank allowed them any fun at all?"

"Oh well, you know, I think a good time should be had by all, *all the time!*" she laughed, "So when one or two of them can sneak out of that hovel village *he* forces them to live in, well, I let them in for free and serve a free drink or three before they have to hurry back to be counted or forced to give *him* energy. Who knows, maybe sometime he will take some of the energy from one of his family members who just left here and get a little tipsy himself!"

"Now that I would pay to see!" A great gut-busting laugh suddenly came over Melvin.

"Anyway," Louise continued moving in closer and becoming very serious, "I believe I got the skinny and it may be of great interest to us all, but I wanted to bounce it off you before I tell the rest of the Council. I have come to the conclusion that it is very likely that just before our Jane was reborn to the material plane, the Xu clan also greeted a child that same day. But, wow! This kid gives me the heebie-jeebies. They called him Po Duk Xu. There is just something different about him. At first, he seemed keen but when I had checked in a few times, I realized that his behavior is just like Jane's. What if, and this is a terrifying thought, Melvin," she grasped his arm as if hanging on for dear life, "but what if, Po Duk Xu can see and hear his family members on our side just like Jane can see and hear us? What if he can hear and see Zank Xu himself? I don't even want to think about the implications."

"You'd better think about 'em," said the increasingly alarmed Melvin, "you'd better bring this to the Council right away!"

CHAPTER X: THE COUNCIL PLAN

Back in the Council room all members were seated at the table except for Levi. He stood leaning on an intricately carved mantle piece and thoughtfully puffed on his pipe.

Gillius spoke first.

"Thank you all for interrupting your afterlives on such limited notice for this Council meeting. Louise has brought most disturbing news to us. Tanquam ex ungue leonem."

"Exactly," puffed Levi, "we do know the lion by his claw. Now we have another piece of this puzzle and the overall picture comes into view. It is only my conjecture at this moment but I believe that somehow Zank Xu has orchestrated the lifting of the veil of all existence that obscures human knowledge of the ethereal plane, in his newest family member. We all know that our individual spirits, or souls if you prefer, our innate individual energies reside in the human mind; or rather in its consciousness." Now pacing the floor he continued. "The barrier that descends in the mind at the moment of rebirth and creates a blockade between the material and the ethereal planes, has somehow been manipulated or ripped through in Po Duk Xu as evidenced by his behavior. I believe it is Zank Xu that is responsible." Levi was clearly becoming angry.

"The questions," posed Caroline, "are why has this happened in our family as well? Is someone in our family also manipulating the veil? How do we use or interpret this new information? We were going to watch Jane from afar and have only Levi interact with her. Is that decision still relevant? Our family has always been ace-high and, according to Hoyle, the decisions we make now will affect us for eternity on both planes of existence."

"You are exactly correct, Caroline," Lucille nodded approvingly, "this family is well respected and without exception the Quintus family motto has been scrupulously followed. I am concerned that this time, in this situation, we still do not know what that 'right choice' is. We have never before been faced with such a dilemma, this is truly unprecedented and we must carefully consider how to proceed."

It was Jacob who pounded the table with his fist and stood with a sudden volatile burst. "After consideration, it should be agreed that we must arm Jane with as much knowledge as possible to prevent her possible molestation by the world around her and quite likely by the Xu clan or even Xu himself. Yes, we are one of the two strongest families. I believe the Universal Energy who sees all has anticipated the dark plan and the evil intentions and actions of Zank Xu and has lifted the veil of all existence in Jane so she can help us protect eternity. There can be no other explanation. She must survive by her wits and take action with our help."

"We must go over the top and do our bit," insisted Melvin. "Jacob's right. Only the Universal Energy could have lifted the veil in Jane and what other reason could there be but to counteract Xu's evil plans. The Universe likes balance. If they got one then we get one, if you get my meaning. "Eternity has become a no man's land and it seems like we and the clan of Zank Xu are the combatants."

"Let us remain wary of overreaction," Gillius stated calmly. "I agree with Jacob and Melvin. There does appear to be a Universal balance in play. I do think it would be wise for you to begin teaching Jane as much as you can, as soon as you can, Levi."

"Perhaps we should all lend our guidance to Jane." Lucille said with a thoughtful glance toward Levi.

Levi looked toward the window and produced a few more puffs of smoke from his pipe.

"There is a decided intelligence present in our Jane. I sense the strong mind of the young woman I knew as Madeline is within Jane as well. I will begin an intensive educational program immediately. Po Duk Xu is the same age as Jane and currently resides on the other side of her world. For the moment she is safe enough in her environment. Let us wait a bit before introducing her to the rest of the family until we get the lay of the land so to speak. We don't want to overwhelm a small child with the responsibility of saving the eternity of her entire family, do we?"

Louise nodded her approval. "I agree with Levi. He is right on the mark. We shouldn't take any chance on denying her a happy childhood. She should have every opportunity to grow into the incredible woman she is meant to be with as much fun and as little drama a possible."

"All right. It is decided," Gillius announced. "We must arm Jane with as much knowledge of the world around her as is possible. Levi will begin Jane's instructions immediately, and the rest of us will watch carefully for any sign the Xu clan is moving toward her." He banged the marble stone on its base with resonance.

Chapter Xi:
The Family

While the Council was working quickly to figure things out on their plane of existence, I was doing my level best to do the same on mine. Of course, my worries were significantly less important than their concerns but they were really big to me. You have probably gathered from stories related by my family members that I learned a lot through observation. I intently watched people to see what they did and how they acted. I knew that attentively scrutinizing life around me was my best method of developing understanding since I could not do much else in my early life. The family get-togethers happened at least once each month, sometimes with my cousins and sometimes only adults would come.

It was at one such gathering that the following questions leapt to mind. I wonder why adults seem to think that small children do not understand them. Weren't they small children at some point? Don't they remember what it was like to have the adults talk about them?

Spring had come early and my family could not wait to begin our cookouts together. On one such occasion, a family picnic was in full swing at our house, and I was sitting in a playpen next to my aunts who were at the large picnic table Dad made the year before. They were chatting the afternoon away. I should say gossiping since that was really their favorite form of entertainment. Aunt Annie said to Aunt Madonna, "It is really unfortunate that Jane isn't as cute or boisterous as Josie is, and that eyebrow is really going to cause her trouble. I wonder when Pauline will do something about it."

Aunt Madonna responded, "You know that Pauline doesn't believe in using any cosmetics or changes in physical appearance no matter how unfortunate her face is. She believes that we should all exist in the way God intended us to live."

"I have an unfortunate face?" I thought to myself. "That doesn't sound like a good thing."

Aunt Madonna continued. "Pauline thinks we should all live and look the way God made us. Joaney has been a real challenge for her on that front and I think Josie and Jane are going to catch the fallout from it. Poor little one; it is so very unfortunate; she has a hard life ahead of her." They all looked over at me with pity in their eyes.

I thought they used that word "unfortunate" an awful lot. I was really beginning not to feel well. My stomach sort of hurt and it felt like there was a lump of something stuck in my throat.

"I should say so," said Aunt Alice, "Jane is just over eighteen months old now and she doesn't speak yet, not even baby babble, there must be something wrong with her mentally too, if you know what I mean." They all nodded "knowingly". "Of course Pauline will never believe it. Nothing is ever wrong with any of her children. They are all perfect! Just ask her, she'll tell you so!"

They all laughed or rather cackled at that description. And then I heard:

"Shhh! Here she comes."

My mother came over with a plate of food and joined her sisters at the table. She looked down at me briefly and smiled. Suddenly they started discussing what a beautiful day it was and how lucky it was the predicted rain showers had held off. How glad they were for the arrival of such an early spring. Surely the planting season would be early as well.

My feelings were really hurt. I don't know why, but I turned my head away from them so they could not see that tears were streaming down my face. I think I didn't want them to know they hurt me. I didn't want to give them the satisfaction of knowing they had so deeply wounded me. I looked around everywhere I could see; I was really hoping for the purple mist and lights to take my attention away from that horrifying conversation.

Unfortunately, instead of the mist I was so hoping for, Grandma approached the table.

My mother's mother was decidedly the family matriarch. I must admit that she scared me. I should explain that last statement. My grandmother was very stern and non-tactile. I would never in my life hug her or be hugged by her. In fact, and this is skipping ahead a few years, at a get-together at Aunt Alice's house, I remember running up to my Grandmother when she arrived. Everyone was paying his or her respects to her for deigning to make an appearance so I thought I should just run up and give her a big hug. My cousins and I had been having a grand time playing in the dirt and I was rather filthy.

"Hi, Grandma!" I said with excitement as I approached her with my arms out. She stopped me dead in my tracks by pointing the tip of her cane squarely at my chest. "Stay right there, sister!" (Grandma called every female sister, especially when she gave orders.) Looking down her nose she continued, "I don't want any dirty child crawling on me!"

Grandma spoke with such authority and sounded so angry (always) she frightened me more than usual. This time she had such an intimidatingly mean look on her face that I burst into tears immediately. I thought your family was supposed to love you no matter what. So what if I was dirty? Couldn't she have found a better way to make her point other than total humiliation and intimidation? But then that was Grandma. She wanted everyone to know exactly where he or she stood with her. Honestly, I don't think she ever had any use for me. But, I will continue that thought at another time. All I had wanted was a hug. I really didn't think that was so much to expect from my grandmother. My mother saw that my feelings were hurt and said that hugging wasn't how Grandma showed affection.

At the time I was not certain how she did show affection or if she was even capable of it. Now I know she took care of her family, her home, the finances of the farm and saved every penny she could. In fact, I believe Grandma spent every waking moment serving and providing for her family. She was the first one up and the last one down, always. No one could outwork Grandma, a fact she took great pride in. I think that was her way of showing she loved us, which is really a guess since she criticized much more than complimented.

I would have to call her harsh in her view of life, but then life had not been fair to her at all. It was like she expected her life to be hard; in fact, she dared life to be hard, because she would meet it head on no matter what. Nothing could defeat her ever. Of course, as she dared it to do so, life obliged her with some tragic challenges. She lost a young daughter to a disease that is now completely curable. The child was only nine years old and medicine at that time had not yet advanced enough to save her. I cannot imagine how unbearably difficult that must have been for her. But there were other children and a husband who required her attention and the farm would not run itself. Grandma took care of everyone and everything that needed her.

There was also the car accident that left her physically bent almost in half. I overheard that the treatment for a crushed pelvis and spine at the time it happened was simply to leave the patient lying in bed and hope everything healed like it was supposed to. She was crippled and in constant pain for the rest of her life. Maybe it was the pain that made her seem so angry all of the time? I cannot say since I did not have the opportunity to know her before the accident. It happened before I was born.

Another less than endearing trait (at least from my perspective) was that Grandma had definite views of how children should behave. I heard her say on more than one occasion that children should be seen and not heard. Grandma was one tough lady who did not suffer foolishness at all.

I should also provide some background and geographical information. My brother James, I believe, mentioned it earlier but, it was Grandma's master plan to give each of her children land when they got married so they would always be around her and Grandpa as they got older. This meant that we all lived in a sort of grid pattern surrounding our grandparents' farm. Each of our homes was separated by a field and across the road from one another. On the north side of Austere Road, there was a field and then my family home, and a field to the west and then Grandma and Grandpa's house. There was another field and the home of Aunt Alice and Uncle Dan and their six boys and then a field and the home of Uncle Anthony and Aunt Minetta and their three kids (two boys and a girl). Across the road from my house was where Aunt Annie and Uncle Hank lived with their four girls. Directly across from Grandma and Grandpa and to the west of Aunt Annie lived Aunt Janet and Uncle Dave and their two girls. Aunt Madonna and Uncle Bob lived with their three boys and a girl in the home across the westerly field from Aunt Janet and directly across the road from Aunt Alice. You get the idea. We were all aligned on the same road and within easy calling distance of the "dreaded whistle".

Allow me enlighten you regarding the dreaded whistle. Whenever Grandmother needed a grandchild to perform some chore for her, she would stand on her front porch and blow a police whistle as loudly as she could. Once a grandchild was deemed old enough by her to be of service, you were expected to drop whatever you were doing and run across the field or road to her presence and complete the task she demanded. From the group that answered her summons, she would select the grandchild or grandchildren she wanted and send the rest home. Grandma didn't always use the whistle, however; on the occasion that she wanted to summon a specific grandchild, she would pick up the phone and call. Most often she would summon my brothers Alvin and James. They were the oldest male grandchildren and therefore of most use to Grandma and

Grandpa. Grandma considered Joaney to be too delicate for farm work so she rarely called upon her. This was just fine with Joaney, who looked upon herself as too much of a princess to actually get dirty. So it worked well between them.

But that is information mostly of future use. But back to the reality of my present situation, I was still sitting in the playpen with my cheeks stained by my tears. I looked to the table and watched my Grandmother holding court with her daughters. I looked back at the rest of the yard where cousins were running around; Dad was cooking on the outdoor grill, shooting the breeze (as he called it) with Uncle Hank, and the volleyball net was strategically placed for a tournament later that day. Finally, to my great relief, the purple, hazy mist appeared, and then a bright dark green beam of light came right down the center and Uncle Levi stepped through.

Chapter XII: The Lessons Begin

The lessons began that very afternoon. Only Uncle Levi could have taken my attention away from the horrible pain of having my feelings hurt.

"Dry your tears, little one." He directed, "We have much work to accomplish and very little time in which to do it." I did not understand what he meant at that particular moment, but from then on Uncle Levi was with me every minute of every day. He chose to teach me by telling me stories and carefully explaining what he said I would need to know.

I asked once, "Why don't anybody else talk to you?"

"Why doesn't anyone else speak with you?" he corrected me. "Because no one else can see me or hear me. I will explain why that is so when you are older, but for now, you must focus on your lessons, young lady. That is your primary task for the time being."

I have thought back often and tried to remember, at any point during my early childhood, of a time when Uncle Levi wasn't around; but from that moment on, it seemed he was always there, even when other people were with me like when Mother would change my clothes or feed me. I cannot think of a time when Uncle Levi wasn't there teaching me. Mother never saw him of course and

I didn't need to speak or use my voice to ask questions so no one else knew he was there but me. I liked that.

At first, Uncle Levi told me stories and used flashcards to teach me very basic things such as numbers and letters. But then the most wonderful thing happened; he could make things appear with flashes of light and the purple, hazy mist. He would use these visual teaching aids, which he called 'view ports' with great ease. To demonstrate 'A' and its use in the English language, he showed a lovely apple tree in an orchard with apples on the ground all around it. We often played word and number games and he seemed quite pleased with how quickly I incorporated the knowledge he provided.

Uncle Levi said, "It would seem that the Universal Energy has seen fit to expand upon the genius you possessed in your previous lifetime, my dear. You have been given a great gift that you must use responsibly." I always promised him I would be responsible, but without really understanding what that meant. Uncle Levi would gently laugh at my assurances. "Some lessons only time can teach," he would say.

Once when we were talking about history, Uncle Levi showed me the destruction of Pompeii as it was happening. It was kind of like Dad showing family movies except I was in the movie and there was no movie screen. He explained that there was no value of time on the ethereal plane so he could show me events as if to me they were happening right then. But, when he saw how much that horrifying scene frightened me and said, "Perhaps we will move on to another topic for now." The scene changed to the Continental Congress and the debates of the founding fathers before the signing of the Declaration of Independence. I liked that subject matter much better. I had seen the Disney movie about Johnny Tremain and the silver smithy but this was completely different. Uncle Levi showed me as it had really been. Their daily life was not as ideal as the movie had made it seem and the participants in the Continental Congress argued a lot less delicately than it had been portrayed in the movies as well.

No matter where I went or what was going on around me, Uncle Levi was there. It was sort of fun when we were riding in the car. Sometimes he would be sitting in the front seat facing me in the back seat. He looked silly with the car seat as his middle. I think he did it on purpose to make me laugh. It was effective. When Uncle Levi was outlandish or entertaining like that it made me forget about the other hurtful things I would hear and I really appreciated that. He worked with me every day, all day and every night until I fell asleep. When I awoke in the morning Uncle Levi was often there, right beside my crib waiting for me to begin again. We discussed many different subjects. Math, chemistry, physics, biology, physical science, English grammar, world literature, many languages, history and geography were all topics of discussion.

He could make most anything interesting. He helped me physically too. In fact, when I was nineteen months old it was Uncle Levi who said, "It is time you should be walking young lady."

I looked at him with inquisitive eyes. "Get up, get up," he said with the strong guttural Dutch accent. I had been sitting on the floor while Mother washed the dinner dishes and cleaned the kitchen. She had been talking to Joaney who was sitting at the kitchen table after dinner becoming very frustrated with her homework. Josie was there too, across from Joaney, coloring on a piece of construction paper. Uncle Levi sat on the floor with me and commanded, "Like this," then he put his hands on the floor and worked his legs underneath him and slowly stood up. I simply repeated the maneuver he had just shown me and was suddenly standing in the middle of the kitchen with no support. I was a bit wobbly at first but very quickly gained may balance. "Wunderbar!" Uncle Levi exclaimed! "Now, move your left foot toward me." I did as I was told. "And now do the same thing with your right foot." Again, I did as I was told. "Come to me child!" he said with such joy in his voice I walked right over to the chair he had sat down upon. "I am so proud of you!" He praised with enthusiasm. I felt a strong connection to Uncle Levi; I always felt safe with him and trusted him completely.

It was a few moments later when I heard my mother say, "Charles! Charles! Come quickly! Jane is walking!" My father and brothers all rushed into the room. Even Joaney and Josie stood up to watch. They were really very excited. It seemed that this walking thing was a pretty big deal. If I had known that, I would have done it a lot sooner.

Chapter XIII:
Josie And The Nursery School Incident

I think it important for you to hear of the next major event from my sister Josie, since apparently it affected her just as much as it did me. It may even have affected her more than me. I didn't mean to cause such a disruption in her world but to be fair, she is right, what happened changed everything permanently.

Jane wasn't really too much of a bother until the nursery school incident occurred. I had successfully out maneuvered her and was still unquestionably the favorite in the family. I was really quite pleased with myself. From people at church and people in the grocery store I heard over and over again, "What a pretty little girl you are!" And it was often followed with, "Oh, how bright your eyes are!" Of course, I knew these were all quality people and so their judgments must be correct. I tried to use my physical beauty and charming personality to stay ahead of the little sister I was forced to accept. I had heard the aunts and uncles say how unlucky it was that Jane wasn't as cute or as personable as I was and that she was going to have trouble in her life because of it. I really hoped the old people were right. Again, when they said it and for just a moment, I thought it was good for me, but I think I realized almost immediately that the grown-ups weren't seeing Jane like I did. I knew that while Jane was quietly and intently watching all that went on around her, she was learning. It was like she observed behavior and happenings and reactions and then filed the information away for future use. Mom was concerned because Jane didn't speak or stand or crawl or walk as early as I did. The family actually thought Jane was slow or mentally challenged. At the very least, they seemed to think she was behind in her ability to learn, but I knew better. I don't know why I knew that, I just did. Maybe, as the older sister, I could look into her like she did me. But I tell you here and now that even when I was four years of age, I knew that Jane, who was then two and a half, was already ahead of all of us. Way ahead.

Mom was a teacher by nature and by profession. She taught music to any one of any age and she was also a certified schoolteacher. She had tried for what seemed like a long time to teach me to read early on. Mom would hold up flash cards with the letters of the alphabet and pictures on them until I knew them by heart. Then we eventually graduated to cards with words and pictures on them. Of course, whenever Mom would have these learning sessions with me, my sister, still a baby back then, was right there by her side, watching and observing, but never saying a word.

And then it happened. The worst day of my life.

Before I tell you what happened, I need to set the scene. I was four when that school year started so I was too young to enter kindergarten and would have to wait until the following September to start. Mom wanted to be sure I was socializing with other children I wasn't actually related to, so she took a job as a pre-school teacher in town. I was enrolled in the class. Ostensibly, the class was for me but, of course, the little sister had to come along too. I suppose two and a half is really too young to be left at home alone, I just wished she could have been sent somewhere else, anywhere else. I wanted time with Mom to myself, so that I could show her just how I could shine, but that was just not to be. So I did what I could with what I had to work with.

I made friends quickly and just as quickly took the lead in every activity. I would make up games, and make up rules to play those games and of course, everyone had to play by my rules. I was really enjoying the whole pre-school experience. Jane stayed firmly planted by Mom's side most of the time. On the occasions when that was not possible because Mom was leading the class in some activity, Jane would play quietly by herself, by putting puzzles together or flipping through the pages of books or playing with the lettered blocks in the activity center. Sometimes I would see her staring off into an area of the room where I didn't see anything happening at all. At first I didn't understand why she stared. Slowly, I realized that she wasn't staring off into space. It was like she was looking at someone or something and observing them, even listening to them. But there was no one there. It didn't make any sense. That is for another time, though; let me get back to the event that literally changed my young life.

It was parents' day at the pre-school. This meant that many of the mothers were there in the classroom observing their children and watching Mom as she taught. They mostly grouped together and talked quietly amongst themselves about their little Stevie or Sandy and how wonderfully he or she was doing in school and how blazingly bright their very intelligent child's future was. It was like they were all saying, "My kid is better than your kid." Of course, I just knew that they were only deluding themselves. None of their kids were better than me at anything and never would be.

After story time, each student was to stand and tell our classmates and parents alike, what we wanted to be when we grew up and why we hoped for that profession or station in life. Each of us stood in turn. There was the standard fireman, policeman, teacher, and mommy. I wanted to be a ballerina so everyone could see me. I even demonstrated my talent with a beautiful pirouette.

While this little circle of indulgence continued, my sister Jane toddled over to the blocks at the activity center that was located in an area of the room between our mother the teacher and the group of mothers hovering and bragging about their own child. When the last student had spoken their mind, one of the mother's smiled down at Jane and said, "what about you little one, what do you want to be when you grow up?" For a moment, Jane looked at her intently, and then without a word, picked up the blocks and placed them on the table in front of her. First, she picked up the letter 'N' and then followed it with the letter 'U'. The mothers were all watching her so the rest of us joined to watch the show too. When she had finished placing the blocks, they said N-U-C-L-E-A-R P-H-Y-S-I-C-I-S-T. The group of women collectively gasped. Our mother came over and looked at the blocks and at my sister and turned really white. I thought she looked really sick, like she might faint on the spot. So I studied the blocks and saw the funny letters Jane had strung together. It didn't look like much of anything to me, but obviously the parents in the room thought otherwise.

Then, Jane did that staring thing again. She looked just to the right of the group of mothers and seemed to be listening to someone I could not see.

Mom bent down to the table and softly said, "Jane, do you know what these blocks say?"

Jane turned from whatever she was looking at and met our mother's eyes. For the first time in her life, Jane spoke. It wasn't a single word answer or baby babble as one might have expected from a toddler who had not yet uttered a single word. Jane's very first attempt to speak in her lifetime came in the form of a complete sentence.

She said, "Of course, mother. I spelled nuclear physicist."

The mothers all gasped again. Then I heard "What a brilliant little girl!"

"You are so blessed to have her!" said one of the mothers who had been watching.

"You must be so very, very proud!" exclaimed another.

I wanted to vomit! I knew my little world of domination had come crashing to an end. My days of being the favorite were over. I had no idea what to do or how to react, and I felt my emotions rising up from my toes swelling all the way up and through my body. It was a power surge of anger the likes of which I had never felt before. I tried really hard to keep it contained, so much so that I started to tremble and then to shake. When, it had welled all the way up to my head, I clenched my fists and stomped my foot and let out a guttural "Aughhh!" I stared at Jane with hatred. At first, I thought she looked right through me, like I didn't matter but then I realized that she had only been looking past me briefly. When our eyes met I could see she seemed to understand how hurt I was. Jane picked up the blocks and put them all away and then tried her best not to be seen by hiding behind our mother. But the damage was already done. The information was already out there. This bell could not be unrung. There was a new superstar in the family and it was definitely not me.

Chapter XIV: Joaney

Joaney thought that since Josie got to tell you about her woes, that she should have the same opportunity. I believed her thoughts might provide an even greater sense of our home life so I didn't object. I did ask her to include her feelings as she could remember them and I got a bit more than I bargained for. I have learned a lot about my sister's perspectives from writing this story and now, I'm afraid, you will too. But it is what it is. No matter how much your family bugs you, they are still your family and you learn to appreciate them for who they are.

"It was never dull having Jane for a sister, that's for sure. You have heard some of this before from other family members, but they didn't relay how these events affected me. I need to tell you about my personal tragedy."

" I never understood why my parents had to adopt another child. In fact, I still do not understand. When they were discussing the application to the agency, I told Mom that I did not think another child was necessary and honestly it was really embarrassing that they were even contemplating the idea."

"My mother was forty when Jane arrived. She should have been done with babies and should have been focusing on me. My friends' mothers didn't have babies around who took *their* attention. *Their* mothers took them shopping and to movies or the theatre. *Their* mothers did what mothers are supposed to do, shop, give advice, and teach their daughters to use make-up."

"My life was already so unfair. *My* mother didn't believe in make-up. She didn't approve of my need to use it and refused to buy it for me. I actually had to get a job so I could afford my own case stocked with the latest shades and textures. There I was, just turned seventeen and in competition with a toddler for my mother's attention, working after school and watching my little sisters. I hated babysitting. That should have been my time to shine, but there was Jane. I couldn't compete with her on any level and my social life was suffering. Could any teenager survive such a difficult home life?"

"My sister's intellectual capacity isn't the only difficulty I had to overcome. Josie mentioned earlier that (before the nursery school incident) Mom thought Jane was developmentally behind because she didn't crawl or stand or walk as early as any of us did. Well, the fact is that she never crawled at all. I guess it was because she had never saw any one else in the house doing it. Josie was already walking when Jane showed up. Any way at nineteen months of age, Jane stood and walked like she had been doing it for years. There was the smallest amount of unsteadiness in her first steps and then she just walked around the house like she owned the place. Our parents were thrilled! Our aunts and uncles and cousins and siblings were amazed, and Jane was the talk of the family from that day on."

"They had all noticed Jane watching them. It could be sort of unsettling at times. But as our mother would say, when asked why Jane wasn't crawling or standing or making some other developmental milestone, "Jane doesn't do anything until she is good and ready to do it." I guess Mom got that right. She walked when she was ready to and not before. It wasn't just the walking, though; Jane was left handed unlike anyone else in the family. At dinnertime, Mom would put a spoon in Jane's right hand and she would always change it over into her left hand. My sister was just different from me in almost every way."

"Once she decided she was physically capable, Jane could do almost anything. At three, she climbed the giant weeping willow in the back yard. Once she learned something, like how to use a whiffle bat she never missed when she swung. Her eye-hand coordination was far superior to my own; but then it was far superior to our brothers too. They thought this was funny at first, but when a three and a half year old starts showing up an eleven year old boy, it just isn't that funny for him anymore.

"James and Alvin pretty much stopped interacting with her. They really didn't want to baby sit for her at all. They liked to play with Josie, though, and they would take her places with them; I really liked the time Josie spent with them. Those were the moments that I could talk to mom about college and boys and hair again and I liked that."

I was really looking forward to college. I wanted to get out of the house and away from the children and finally live with people my own age that saw life like I did. I couldn't wait. I remember thinking just one more year and I would be free! What a wonderful daydream that was. Mom was apprehensive about my leaving but she knew I was determined. I know family is the most important thing in the world, but sometimes getting away from family and flying solo is just as important. And I was really, really ready, even desperate for a break.

Section III: Friends And Enemies

I have told you much of what was going on in the lives of my sisters and myself and until now have let ethereal side of the story unfold in bits and pieces. Please remember, all of these events were occurring simultaneously. While Joaney was headed off to college and Josie was trying to reestablish her dominance, my family on the ethereal plane was keeping close tabs on everything everywhere that might affect me. That was no small feat even for them.

Chapter Xv:
The Report

Back on the ethereal plane, a meeting took place at the dwelling Gillius had created as his private residence. Melvin and Lucille arrived to discuss the information collected regarding the observations of the Xus on the physical world and the scuttlebutt compiled by friends and family on the ethereal plane, most of which came from Louise's speakeasy.

The home of Gillius Quintus was fairly typical for the time in which he had lived. It had red tiles on the roof and was made of brick. Everything inside the home was centered on a beautiful courtyard that Gillius took great pleasure in creating and sustaining. There was a lovely colorful floor mosaic and a few paintings on the walls but the furniture was sparse at best. To accommodate his guests, Gillius added some seats that really looked more as if they were meant to lounge on than to sit on. As a final touch of hospitality he supplied a few pillows in case his guests felt the need to rest.

He wore what appeared to be a white woolen tunic without the outer garment as this was his usual attire at home. Gillius began, "Sit, sit and let us hear of any new developments."

"Caroline is monitoring the home of Po Duk Xu and Jacob is watching his father's corporation through their view ports into the material plane," reported Lucille.

"And Louise is keeping her ear to the ground at her gin joint for any information she can pick up from the Xu family members on our side," added Melvin.

"Caroline has seen that Po Duk still occasionally acts as if he is talking to someone that she cannot see. It is possible that someone from our side is interacting with him as Levi is with Jane. It is odd though that Caroline cannot determine who it may be. If someone here is communicating with the boy they are hiding their energy from us," Lucille said with concern.

"Odd indeed," considered Gillius. "It would take someone with great power to obscure their energy from our view ports. Actually, it is a fine idea. A useful protection measure, I should have thought of it myself. But only the energy of the person interacting with the boy is obscured and not the child's home?"

"Yes," said Lucille, "that is certainly the case."

"Very interesting," said Gillius, thinking out loud. "Either Xu is not as powerful as anticipated or he is hiding his activities in plain sight hoping we would not notice. Hmm. What about the father's place of business?"

"Jacob reports no abnormal activity of any kind," Lucille replied. "The father does not seem to be involved in any way."

"Louise tells me she is letting the drinks flow freely for any Xu clan member who may sneak in for some temporary relief from their plight," Melvin informed the group. "You know how happy and sociable her energy tonic can make you feel. It seems the Xus need lots of help to relax and they slam down those joyful concoctions just as quickly as they can. Her patrons mostly have more rumor than detail, but it does seem like one of their family members disappears just before Po Duk is seen to interact with the invisible presence. I have compared notes of information from Louise with Caroline and it happens every time. A few of his clan are questioning whether Zank Xu is sacrificing their energy to the dark force of the Abyss in order to gain more power to visit the material plane. I don't think he can step through like we can. It seems like he needs some extra help. But the scariest of the rumors she's heard is that some say he even possesses his family members on the physical world. But it's only speculation at this point."

"That is frightening speculation indeed." Gillius was becoming much more uneasy.

Melvin nodded knowingly and continued. "Louise also told me that the first advisor to Xu is a frequent visitor to her place and speaks a lot more freely than he should, 'specially after a drink."

Gillius was pensive. "Hmmm." He seemed to be considering or formulating a plan. "I believe it is advisable that Louise should make every effort to reach out to the first advisor. If he feels comfortable with her, he may open up and provide more information than he already has. To have knowledge supplied from someone so close to Xu himself is wholly invaluable."

" Now," he said has he stood up, "I must go and speak with a trusted friend; please let us all continue our diligent efforts. There can be no rest until the danger has been quashed."

Chapter Xvi:
The Struggles Of Zank Xu

Sooner or later we were going to have to get back to the villain of the story. That time has arrived. I assure you that the information provided is an accurate compilation of first hand witnesses accounts in the palace of Xu of the ethereal realm. What follows are the events as I have been told they actually occurred.

Zank Xu sat on a golden emperor's throne with deep imperial red crushed velvet and silk upholstery in the opulent quarters he created. A black swirling mist surrounded him momentarily and then wafted to a new location where it would hover again until his mood shifted. His advisors had learned that whenever he was anxious, this black mist would appear so they knew not to disturb him unless summoned or they would certainly face some dire consequences.

He had opened a view port to the material realm to monitor the goings on there. As he viewed his family and the happenings of what he considered his earthly dominion, he was *very* anxious. He desperately needed to find a better way to impact the existence of his family members. He needed to take control. To accomplish the level of domination he wanted, he needed to draw more energy out of those under his ethereal control. He rubbed his furrowed brow with his long thin fingers and reached for a golden goblet of the energy-strengthening elixir (as he called it) that was placed on his table beside him.

The cup was empty.

"Aaghh!" he exclaimed in instant rage and frustration. He demonstrated his aggravation with a powerful wave of his hand. The cup flew across the room and slammed into the wall opposite him leaving a dent in the gilded woodwork of his luxurious space.

"Is there no one in this family who is capable of the simplest task?" He bellowed with great fury. "Is there a single soul with the sensibility of a stone? Why do fools and imbeciles surround me? It is no wonder I have not been able to gain the power I seek, my advisors are idiots!" Anger and rage contorted his face and body while the black mist swirled almost at hurricane speed.

"I am forced to step into only the most susceptible morons to control any part of my family on the material plane. Their power is so limited it is almost not worth my considerable effort. If I were able to take them over long enough, I would help them rise through the leadership of what amounts to little more than the corporate gangs this family has been reduced to, and would eventually have more power myself. It is a long and arduous process and it uses great amounts of my strength. My recovery each time is longer and more difficult. Is it too much for my advisors to keep my cup full?"

Just as the last word of his tirade leapt from the lips of Zank Xu, the first of his advisors rushed in with a pitcher of elixir. He retrieved the cup from its landing spot on the floor and nervously filled it to the rim. The advisor (known only as the first) struggled with his long cloak as he hurried across the room with both pitcher and cup in his hands. He indelicately and unceremoniously tripped and tumbled to the feet of Zank Xu, spilling everything he carried.

A second advisor (aptly called the second, of course) entered immediately, carrying another pitcher of elixir and an identical goblet. He did not fall as he approached the master. He calmly and silently placed the cup on the gilded and ornately carved table at the side of the throne and filled it with elixir. He bowed deeply to show his respect and exited the same way he had entered.

The first advisor scrambled to make amends for his error.

"I am terribly sorry, your Greatness!" He squealed in pleading tones as he scurried to clean up the mess. Once the items were secured and the elixir removed he prostrated himself at the foot of the throne. "I humbly beg your majestic forgiveness, Master," he whimpered.

Zank Xu looked down at the inept advisor with utter disgust. With only cold hatred in his voice he said, "You are not worthy of my presence, you blundering waste of energy. Return to your inadequate and impoverished hovel! I will deal with you later. Get out of my sight!"

The swirling black mist suddenly attacked and enveloped the groveling advisor who made choking, gasping and gagging noises while his body contorted with agony as he dissolved from view.

"Well, now I need a new advisor," Xu thought, as he stroked his goatee. He closed his eyes and sat back in his throne. In his mind he searched his family energy for a suitable replacement servant, who may earn the title of advisor to his Greatness. "To whom shall I extend the honor?" he thought. He searched each of the shacks he had so generously allowed family members to create for themselves. He had been very careful to be certain that as each spirit entered the ethereal plane they first appeared before him and learned the rules of existence in his family domain

1. Never at any time should they hold their head be higher than his. No matter his position, standing, seated or lying down, they must

always appear smaller than he.

2. The space they create for themselves must never be of any consequence or in any way remarkable. If they tried to add any comforts he had not thought to allow them to include himself, their home would be destroyed and their energy severely punished.
3. Their clothing would be long and baggy and appear to be made of burlap. They must never believe themselves to be important enough to wear clothing that was either impressive or comfortable as they would never be as important as he. The fourth rule was the most important of all.
4. When summoned to his presence they must appear at once and if deemed worthy to be called to be his servant they must accept that role or the punishment would be both immediate and severely painful.

Zank Xu had learned that as much as he would sometimes have liked to, he was incapable of the total destruction of the energy of family members. This was probably a good thing since he would likely have few members left to rule. He did, however, have the ability to inflict harsh and painful punishments on those that disappointed him. He considered the regularity of these punishments to be necessary to the morale of his family. It was vital to family harmony that each soul learned his or her place and more importantly *his*. As each entered the ethereal plane he greeted them with pain, anguish and torment so they would immediately abide his wishes and accept his power and control.

He periodically searched the homes of his family members to be certain there were no violations of his rules and to remind each of them individually of his superiority. This time however, he was looking for someone with some intelligence that would eventually serve as his advisor. There were a number of newer inhabitants of the ethereal plane; he just needed to sort through them. He decided to retire to his sitting room to think.

He waived his long fingers in a dismissive gesture and the room disappeared in a swirl of black haze and mist.

Chapter XVII: Josie – Much Ado About Jane

Just to keep you up to date with what was happening in my little corner of the universe: Josie thought she should tell you about some people from the Educational Testing System that visited us at home.

"Our older sister, Joaney had gone off to college by this time. She would come home during breaks and ask Mom to help her with her schoolwork. She was behind in almost every class. Jane was usually wherever Mom was so she naturally sat in the tutoring sessions with Joaney. Jane would read the books that Joaney had brought home from school. Yes, I said read. It had been well established at two and a half that my sister could read and comprehend what she was reading.

She began kindergarten at five years old just like the rest of us, but the school quickly contacted our parents and told them Jane just did not belong in class with the rest of the kids. It was very important to Mom and Dad that we grow socially as well as academically (maybe even more important) and so they had intended for Jane to go through the school system just like every other normal kid.

But Jane wasn't normal.

Finally, after much debate with the school board and teachers and with each other, Mom and Dad had taken her to this place to have her educationally tested. I don't know what the results officially were, but I can guess. When they returned from the meeting where they were given the results of the tests, both Mom and Dad looked seriously shaken yet also very proud. I don't think they knew what to do with her either. Anyway, none of this was news to me.

Right after this, I had found Jane in the basement, in our mother's "library" the place where she kept every book she had ever owned. I had found her reading one of Mom's special "Great Books". I guess it was part of a collection of works by historically important authors. I can say that now; but at the time I only knew we were not supposed to touch those books. They were off-limits. We all knew it too, but there was Jane, reading one of the forbidden texts. So I said, "I'm gonna tell Mom!" in hopes of getting Jane to jump up and put the book away while begging me not to relay the information. I was sure I had something to hold over her for blackmail purposes now; but Jane just looked at me almost like she pitied me. I, of course, ran and told our mother that Jane had gotten into her bookshelves.

Mom went down the basement and saw my little sister sitting on the floor reading a book that was almost as big as she was and laughed."

She said, "What are you reading Jane?"

To which my sister responded, "David Copperfield, Mother."

"She always called Mom "Mother". The adults in the family thought it was just precious. It made me want to throw up every time I heard it. When Mom and Jane started discussing the book she was reading and its philosophical importance, I ran out of the room.

It wasn't too long after the book episode that a well-dressed man and woman came to our door. I remember they spoke to Mom alone, because Dad was at the factory where he went to work at every day.

They were very cordial and friendly, almost too much so. I had spent much time mastering my ability to manipulate adults by facial expressions and friendly cuteness. As I sat on the stairs that overlooked the formal living room where our parents entertained guests, I scrutinized them with great interest. It seemed to me that these people, who identified themselves as being with the testing center our parents had taken my sister to, were not what they seemed to be. I thought they were putting on an act trying to be too friendly and too complimentary to our mother. They desperately wanted to meet Jane. I don't know if Mom saw it too or if she just didn't want to take any action regarding "the children" while Dad was away, but she said, "I won't be able to make any decisions right now, will you please leave your names and contact number so I may call you to schedule an appointment when my husband is home? We try to address any issues concerning the children together." I could tell that they were disappointed with her response. The man seemed like he was going to try to pressure Mom into agreeing with whatever it was they were talking about."

"Certainly you must see, Mrs. La Roi, the delicacy of your daughter's situation. She will only be this young for such a short period of time. Our educators very much prefer to begin molding young genius as early as possible. If you would only listen to our presentation."

But the woman interrupted him. "It is quite alright if you are not able to speak with us right now dear." She said reassuringly. "I know you and your husband will make the best decision for Jane. Please feel free to contact us at your earliest convenience. We do so look forward to hearing from you!" She smiled a truly disingenuous smile and thanked Mom for her time. She also promised to remain in touch and to call again later to schedule an appointment. I could see her response put Mom at ease. They got up and headed for the door.

"I ran to my older sister's bedroom window that overlooked the driveway. Mom had stayed inside the house with the glass door closed so she could not hear what they said next, but I opened my window so I could."

"What are you doing?" the man demanded. "Did you see the sister? She was just about crawling out of her skin hoping we'd take the little genius right then. I know I could have convinced the mother to let us have that kid."

"No, not from this one," the woman calmly and quietly responded. "She may look timid, but I bet she's a quiet lioness type and there is no way she'd let that girl out of her sight."

"When they pulled out of the driveway, Mom went to the phone, which was ringing. It was Grandma calling from next door. She wanted to know who was at our house and what they wanted. Mom could not wait to tell her just what had happened."

Chapter XVIII:
The Council Decides To Intervene

Uncle Levi had been standing there near my sister Josie watching the whole incident with the people from the educational testing system. He seemed really quite pleased that my mother had sent them on their way. I don't think he trusted them at all, but he wouldn't tell me why. Anyway, I didn't know it at the time but Uncle Levi wasn't the only one watching out for me. The plan was that, while Jacob, Caroline and Louise were monitoring the Xu clan's movements; Gillius and Lucille maintained surveillance over my family as well.

They had seen that my academic education was progressing very well, far beyond anyone's expectations and they were quite pleased with Levi's efforts. The only difficulty they feared was that I was far more connected to Levi than to my family on the material plane. I was of school age now and they thought that I needed to interact with children in my classroom and with the adults who were or would become important in my life. In short, they knew that I must be able to function in society. As it was, I barely interacted with my immediate family.

At a council meeting with everyone present, Lucille broached the subject.

"I am concerned," she began cautiously, "that our little Jane isn't talking to her sisters or brothers or cousins as much as she should. How will she ever learn to interact with her peers if she cannot or does not interact with her family? She spends all of her time with Levi. She is learning much from him but not the social skills she should learn from actual human physical, mental, and emotional interaction. I believe it may be time that Levi allow her some space on the material plane to grow and develop."

"Wait! Before we decide to do that, what are we going to do about teaching her to be a girl and all that entails?" Caroline brought up. "There is so much to see and do and she is going to need to present herself as a competent woman. Levi just cannot help her with that. Louise and you and I *can*, Lucille. I would like to make a motion that all women of the council be allowed to interact with Jane to help guide her along these lines."

"And what of the men in the family?" Jacob burst out. "I possess great survival skills and insight. Gillius holds incredible diplomatic abilities, and everyone here has had full measure of how charming and persuasive Melvin can be. Is not each of these talents skills that Jane will require? Especially now before Zank Xu raises his pointy, ugly head? I move that it is time all members are introduced to Jane along with our particular skill sets and allowed to interact with her to help her as she needs."

"Point of order," stated Gillius in a calm deep baritone voice, "We cannot have two motions before the council simultaneously. We shall address the first motion by Caroline."

"Hmm." Levi, who had been sitting quietly smoking his pipe, vocalized his thoughts. "If Lucille's motion is to be set aside for the moment, then isn't the point of order really that both Caroline's and Jacob's motions are really the same? It seems that each of you would very much like to be part of Jane's life. I cannot blame or fault any one here as I must say my time with her has been extraordinary and truly fulfilling. I agree it is the best course that each of us teaches what we have learned over our many lifetimes. The question becomes how to allow everyone access without overwhelming her. I, of course, feel her continued academic education is paramount, but I concede the necessity of her development as a woman," he nodded to Caroline, "with both diplomacy and survival skills. It is clear that her best interests require that we share Jane's time."

"All in favor of each member of the Council teaching Jane his or her best skill or talent, signify agreement by saying 'aye'," Gillius declared with authority.

A chorus of hardy 'ayes' filled the room.

"All opposed to the motion of Council interaction with Jane, signify disagreement by saying 'nay'."

Not a sound was heard.

"I declare the motion unanimously passed." Gillius banged the polished and honed marble stone upon its matching marble disk.

"Now it behooves us to find some sort of schedule for each of us to meet with Jane. Levi, you must introduce each one of us so she will know it is safe to accept us and to speak with us."

"Agreed," Levi nodded and puffed on his pipe. "Yes, I believe that is the safest course of action for everyone. Perhaps Louise should be the first as she is female and as Jane has mentioned, 'sparkly'. I anticipate her interest in your clothing would be a likely ice breaker." (This last part he said with obvious amusement.)

"So it shall be," came the booming baritone of Gillius as he again banged the marble stone on its marble disk base.

The room dissolved into a purple mist.

Chapter XIX: Grade School Begins

While the council was working out plans to allow everyone to become involved in my life, I was struggling with the looming first day of grade school. When that big day finally arrived, I found that I was not filled with hopeful anticipation as I expected, but rather I felt much dread and fear mostly thanks to Josie. The day did start out pleasant enough, but quickly changed into a nightmare. Some days it just doesn't pay to get out of bed.

"Get up, Jane! Wake up, Josie!" Mother called out cheerfully the first Tuesday after Labor Day. "It's the first day of a new school year!" The clanging of an old school marm's brass handbell greeted us to join the day. Mom loved that bell. She took great delight in waking us with it every day.

The grass was green and the sun was shining and the sweet smell of the fresh clean air of country life wafted through the open window in our upstairs bedroom. My sister Josie and I shared a bedroom and a bed. Our parents thought it would help us get along better as sisters and since Mom had made Joaney's bedroom into her dedicated sewing area the little brick house really did not have the space for us each to have our own room.

"Get up!" Josie said as she kicked me awake.

"Ow!" I said loudly

"Stop it!" I yelled after she kicked me again.

"I'm telling Mother!" I admit I whined a little when I made that threat. My leg hurt and I was rubbing Josie's footprint off of it.

"You are so weird!" Josie said with disgust. "You talk in your sleep and you were talking to people who don't even exist. What's wrong with you?"

"I am not weird! You don't know what you're talking about! *"Shut up!"* I yelled back at her while still rubbing my leg.

"Freak!" She screamed it at me with such anger it scared me.

I started to cry. "I am not a freak! What's a freak?"

We started to pull on our parochial school uniforms. They consisted of white button up blouses with rounded collars and red, gray and black plaid jumpers. There was a school crest on the left side. I thought it made us look sort of official.

"Someone who doesn't fit in with everybody else." Josie hissed her answer with vehemence. "You *are too* a freak and I cant believe I have to go to school with you. What if the other kids find out you're my sister? I'll never live it down! My life is ruined! *Freak!"*

I cried loudly enough that Mother came to the room.

"What is going on up here? Jane, what is wrong?"

I sniffled and sobbed but finally got out, "Josie called me a freak."

"Well, she is!" Josie said defiantly with her hands on her hips for emphasis.

"Am I a freak?" I asked our Mother in earnest.

"Of course not. You are very special Jane and Josie you know better than to call your little sister names."

"Oh that's right, Jane is soooo special. I wish she would be special somewhere else. I wish she weren't my sister." Josie was absolutely insolent.

"Josie!" Mom exclaimed. "What a horrible thing to say. You don't mean it! Apologize to your sister and tell her you love her."

"I will not! I do mean it! You don't know how awful it is going to be with her at school. I will be an outcast because of her! It's not fair!" That time Josie stomped her foot and crossed her arms for emphasis.

I cried even harder.

"I don't want to go to school" I sobbed. "They are going to be mean to me, they won't like me, even my own sister doesn't like me." I sobbed some more.

"You are both being silly," Mother said in a consoling tone. "You two are just nervous because it's a new experience and a new school year. You will see there is nothing to be afraid of or to worry about. A lot of your classmates are having the same anxiety right now and their parents are telling them the very same thing. Now finish getting dressed and come downstairs for breakfast. The bus will be here soon."

Josie shot me an angry glare as Mother left the room to return to the kitchen. I continued to cry softly as I tried to put on my new school socks.

"I hate you," Josie hissed. "You better not tell anybody we're related. You better not even look at me on the bus. Don't think I'm going to sit next to you or talk to you. I don't want anything to do with you...understand?"

I nodded my head and shuddered as I sniffled. I wanted to throw up. I was so scared and there was no one there to help me. I was certain the first grade was going to be hideously painful. I felt so alone. Mother didn't understand and Josie was so mean. Where was Uncle Levi? I needed him so desperately.

Chapter Xx: An Escape From Zank Xu

At the same time the Council was trying to divide up my time and I was suffering through the first year of grade school, Zank Xu had chosen his new advisor. He was designated as the new third and the previous advisors from the original group each moved up one title. The former second was the new first and the former 3rd became the new 2nd advisor. Zank Xu was very pleased with the labels he conferred upon these souls. He thought they should stand apart from the rest of the family, but not enough to use actual names.

"I like it here! I love it here! This must have been what Camelot looked like to Arthur and Guinevere," the elated newest advisor proclaimed as he entered the palace of Xu.

"And what do *you* know of Camelot?"The new first advisor scoffed at the new third.

"I have read a great deal!" The third boasted. "I *was* a librarian on the material plane, you know. I dare say my literary knowledge is quite extensive."

"Be quite! We don't want to awaken him!" imparted the now second to the new third advisor.

The first chimed in, using a stern but hushed tone to both of his counterparts, "*Quiet!*" and directly to the new third he said, "You stay here!"

The first and second advisors carefully and cautiously approached the room from where their former colleague had been banished. Even though his energy was still in existence, a harsh punishment such as his was, from the powerful Zank Xu could be guaranteed to leave some plasma like drippings behind. The new third advisor ignored the warning and moved right along with them. He was much too excited to stay behind in the outer hallway as he had been instructed.

"I have heard the great master is capable of exceptional vision and perceives many things. What sort of things has he been seeing?" the newest advisor inquired without whispering.

Suddenly a hand with a vice-like grip covered his mouth. It was the new second attempting to get him to understand that he needed to be quiet.

"Like knights in armor," came a whispered reply from the first.

"Knights in armor? Now you are teasing, perhaps trying to make me look foolish? I can believe it if you see knights, or if the second sees knights, but I cannot believe that *he* sees knights. Surely you are joking."

The advisors to Zank Xu were quietly trying to clean the mess left after their previous comrade was removed from their master's throne room.

The second enlightened his newest colleague. "The master reads the stars of the material plane and the energy fields of the ethereal plane. He has long studied these things. He often sees what we do not. He knows what you are thinking right now. He exiled our former first using such tremendous force not only as a punishment for him but also to serve as a reminder to us that he is in charge and is more powerful than we will ever be."

"That may be," replied the new third advisor. "However, before I was summoned to the Master's presence to serve him, I heard that the former first had escaped the confines of his hovel."

"He escaped?" The new first asked. "I thought he was locked up tight. Are you certain he has escaped?"

"Certain? No, I am not certain, but that is the rumor," the third advisor imparted. "We have heard that not only has he escaped the hovel dwelling in which the Master declared he should continue his existence for eternity, but that he has runaway into another family's energy to hide." He was becoming excited at the fact that he had important information that the other advisors were unaware of. It made him feel important. "Rumor also has it that this family was strongest during the period of the Middle Ages when knights and ladies were the 'in crowd'." He made a gesture with the first two fingers on each hand to signify quotation marks. "Say, I wonder if that is why the Master is seeing knights in his visions?"

The first remarked, "Funny you should mention Camelot; do you know where the former first is hiding? The Master will bless us all if we find him and turn him in."

The second advisor added accusingly, "It *was* you who first mentioned Arthur and Camelot. I may not be as well read as you but I do know that story is about knights. Do you know this family or how the former first escaped? Do you know who helped him? The Master will be most pleased if you do." The second added as if he were trying to bribe the information from the new third.

He did not know why but the new third was suddenly wary of being set up. Nervously he replied as if making a formal statement. "I have absolutely no knowledge of the whereabouts of the former first,"

He declared loudly and in a manner that sounded like he might be testifying in a court of law. "I did not mean to imply otherwise. I most humbly beg your forgiveness if I have given any other impression. It was not my intention to do so. I offer myself to help in the search for him if you think my help might be of any value."

"Now there is a useful idea," crackled the voice from the throne. Zank Xu had been listening and only pretending to be asleep. "It is about time one of my advisors had an idea with some merit. *Hmmm.*" He made a long breathy sound as if he were still contemplating whether or not to impart the next piece of information. Suddenly, Zank Xu was no longer sitting on his throne deep in thought. He was standing directly in front of his trio of advisors. He was lording over them seemingly getting taller with each word. He had moved so quickly, there was a trail of blackness still lingering along the path he had taken.

"It is true that the former first has escaped. He did so with the help of culprits as yet unknown to me, but I assure you I will discover their identity." His bony finger moved from advisor to advisor to emphasize his point. "Oh yes, I will most certainly uncover who it is that dares to defy me, and I will all but eradicate them and their family from the ethereal plane when I do. For now, I direct you three to create a search party together to find the disloyal former advisor. Do not return to my presence until you do! Oh, and remember, if you report falsely or should you waste time on a 'wild goose chase',*[mockingly, he dramatically made the air quotations with his fingers in the same manner as the new third had done]*, I will take apart your energy photon by photon."

The advisors bowed as low to the floor as they possibly could go without actually prostrating themselves. Zank Xu waived his long thin hand from the wrist in a dismissive gesture and the advisors scurried from the room.

"Not to worry my brothers," the second advisor began. "I *do* have information on the location of our former comrade in hiding, and more importantly, I have heard a rumor that even the Master does not yet know!"

"Why did not you tell us this before?" asked the first. "You could have saved us from that frightening scene with the Master! You must know he could banish us all!"

"When I came into possession of the information, it was not our place to interfere, it was not our job to do, but now it is," the second replied rather smugly.

"If you know where he is, should not we simply go and extract him?" the third advisor inquired. "I am not frightened of any other family's energy nearly as much as I am of His Greatness; why not just go and take him and bring him back to the Master?"

"Of our group, I have been held as captive…I mean advisor to the Master the longest," began the first. I can tell you that I have learned that the saying 'courage should always be tempered with caution' is absolutely true." He made an attempt to put one of his hands on a shoulder of each of the other advisors, but missed and ended up grabbing both their collars causing them to strangle slightly. "Do you know how many souls there are guarding the former first, if any are guarding him at all? Do you know the layout of the hiding place? Do you know why this family feels they should protect our fallen comrade? It may be that if they feel their loyalty to him is strong, the three of us simply will not be enough to 'just take him' as you have suggested. If the second's information is accurate, we need to complete a bit of reconnaissance before we can act."

"You are right! There may be more souls helping the former first than the three of us can handle. We may need reinforcements." The second agreed.

"I don't understand. Why would any other family help the former first?" asked the third. "Why would they invite the wrath of the Master against their family in order to help him? It just doesn't make any sense to me," he said while shaking his head.

"A fair question!" came a booming disembodied voice from all around them. They all fell to the ground and shook in fear.

"What is it you are not telling me, second? Think carefully about what happened to my former first before you answer."

"I beg your mercy, Master! I will tell you everything I know," pleaded a sniveling second. "I was told by the former first that the Quintus family may have a child born to them on the material plane with the same abilities as Po Duk. Rumors have been swirling about the ethereal plane that a female child was born the same day as Po Duk, in fact within minutes of his birth. The family group we believe to be hiding the former first are allies of the Quintus family. I cannot say for certain, but I think it is reasonable to believe that they are helping the former first in order to gain information from him so they may provide that same information to Gillius Quintus himself. I…I did not wish to bother you with this, Master, because I have no concrete evidence that any of it is true. It may be only the fanciful wonderments or embellishments of a jealous or angry soul. Please, Master, your mercy I beg!"

Chapter XXI: A Frank Conversation With Uncle Levi

Uncle Levi had told me of the Council's plan to introduce each member to me at some point in time, but as he reminded me, time has no meaning on his side of life so I wasn't surprised that they didn't race to meet me by what I guess I would call mortal standard time. What seemed like forever to me was probably less than a day to them or at least that's what I told myself and Uncle Levi more or less agreed.

I had gone through a few years of grade school and was now in the fourth grade. It was torture. The other kids were mean to me because of my eyebrow and it seemed like my sister Josie tried to crush my feelings at least twice each day. I had no inclination to open myself up to any more ridicule than I was already subjected too so I tried not to give any more information about myself than was absolutely necessary. By this stage of the game, I was well aware that children often have the ability to turn any personal knowledge into teasing material. Unfortunately, one day at the very beginning of the new school year my teacher, Miss Starling, asked me to speak to the class about being an adopted person.

"What do you mean, Miss Starling?" I asked. "What is there to discuss?"

Miss Starling was very young for a teacher. In fact, this school year was her very first full time teaching assignment ever. She had just graduated from college and my class was her very first job.

"I thought it might be interesting for your classmates to understand how you came to be part of your family." She said this with such cheerfulness that I didn't want to disappoint her and, besides, everyone was already looking at me.

"Well," I began.

"Please stand up, Jane. We must all remember to stand when we are addressing the whole class." Miss Starling practically cheered at me.

So, I stood up at the side of my desk and everyone turned in their seats to get a better look at me.

"I was adopted," I said. "That means that I am the biological child of people other than my parents. My parents petitioned the Court to raise me as their own child and legally adopted me into their family." I thought I had stated the matter plainly enough. But of course, there was always one person in class I could count on to embarrass me whenever the opportunity presented itself.

"Wait," came a voice from the other side of the room. It was the one voice I didn't want to hear. It was none other than Lori Dizzertelli, the meanest girl in class. She was of Northern Italian decent so she had long blonde hair with just the perfect curl and blue eyes. All the boys in class fawned over her and all the girls, except for me naturally, wanted to be her. I just wanted to stay out of her way. And yet, here I was squarely in her crosshairs. The teasing gun was fully locked and loaded and Lori pulled the trigger.

"So your real mom and dad didn't want you?" she crowed with true glee in her voice.

"My parents are my real mom and dad," I retorted.

"*No*, you just said your real parents gave you away! They probably saw your eyebrow and screamed!" She laughed. "You are so ugly they gave you away 'cause they couldn't stand to look at you!" The classroom erupted into laughter.

"*Lori!*" Miss Starling said in exasperation. "That was absolutely unnecessary! I am so sorry, Jane; I thought that your classmates might be mature enough to discuss the matter of adoption. I guess I was wrong. Please take your seat. We will move onto something else."

I sat back in my seat, totally humiliated. Lori was right; I was ugly. Josie was right, I am a freak; she never missed a chance to remind me of it. But wait, doesn't that make Josie a freak too? I suddenly had the most wonderful thought. Josie was adopted just like I was. If I'm a freak, so is she! I felt so much better; I even smiled to myself.

On the bus ride home, I thought more about being adopted into a family. That meant I wasn't genetically related to any of my family members. But Uncle Levi said I have access to all members of our family on the ethereal plane. I wondered if he meant my genetic family members or my adopted family members. I decided to ask him as soon as I could.

That evening after dinner, after I had fed the dog and taken out the garbage, I waited patiently for Uncle Levi to appear.

"I don't understand, Uncle Levi, are you part of my genetic family or of my adopted family?"

"Both. You see, Jane, you are the bridge or rather the connection that brings all of our energies together. Because of you, our family is that much stronger on both planes of existence. You have united your adopted and genetic families for eternity. As each of them passes to the ethereal plane, they will join with our family because of their connection to you."

"So you're saying that when I cross to the ethereal plane, I will still have to see my sister? And my grandmother?" I was suddenly afraid to hear the answer.

"Absolutely." Uncle Levi did not mince words. "And you will love them even more than you are able to on this plane and they will love you even more as well. You will understand someday."

"Gosh," I stammered, "I was kind of hoping that I could eventually get away from them. Grandma always seems so mean and angry and Josie just takes absolute delight in torturing me."

Calmly and evenly, Uncle Levi said, "I know it seems quite difficult right now at your stage of development, but even you must admit that you love them despite what you see as flawed relationships. You wouldn't wish them any harm would you?"

"Well okay," I answered truthfully, "I suppose I do love them, which does not make any logical sense. No, I don't wish them any harm. I just wish they were nicer to me. I wish they could see me for who I am. But they don't know what I know and they can't see what I see."

"Ahh, there it is!" he said with enthusiasm, like I had just learned to ride a bike or something. "That is the definition of love. You love them and wish them well no matter what the circumstance. You know they do not understand you, but maybe you don't understand them either? Perhaps you should give that some thought?"

"Well," I began, "Grandma is so set in her mind about everything. She is so rigid in her beliefs. If I bring up something that is outside her realm of accepted knowledge, she just shuts me down and makes me feel like I'm some horribly foolish person for even considering or mentioning what I know to be true. She tells me I should be quiet and learn my place. I don't know what to do about that. And Josie, wow, she is mean to me and likes to play jokes on me. She demands I do chores for her and likes to make fun of me. I think its so she can feel smarter and more important. I don't get it. I'm smarter; she's prettier. That's just how it is, so what? Why can't she just accept that we each have different good points and leave it at that? Is she trying to make me feel bad because I am smarter? Is she trying to make herself feel better by making fun of me?"

"Hmmm, both I suppose." Uncle Levi reflected. "What you need to understand my dear is that love will overcome these issues and any others you may have with family members on this plane. When you all get to the other side, none of these things will matter. There is only love and understanding in our family."

"It would be nice if none of these things would matter *now*, on this plane. Why do we have to wait to cross over?" I asked in earnest.

"The troubles and challenges we face on the material plane help us grow and develop and strengthen our energy on the ethereal plane. We join our energies together for strength and grow as a family in love. There are other families on the ethereal plane that do not accept the premise of love but rather use the energy of other members to gain power or at least what they perceive to be power." Uncle Levi was very serious now. "It is time you knew of Zank Xu. He is a dark soul and our family's nemesis."

"Wait, we have a family rival on the ethereal plane? I thought it was supposed to be all hearts and flowers over there?" I said with some incredulity.

"We must all make choices and we have freedom of choice even on the ethereal plane. Our family, for example, has chosen to live in peace and harmony with each other and with the many of the other families we are not yet connected to. We learn and we grow and help each other. So that when we are reborn, we might also help each other on this plane. You see, some remnants of the ethereal plane remain with each of us during every incarnation on this plane. We do not remember our previous lifetimes or our time on the ethereal plane, but some character traits and innate knowledge and skills remain with us from lifetime to lifetime. In your case, for example, it's your great intellect that has grown from lifetime to lifetime and has now surpassed everyone's greatest expectation."

The look on my face must have been one of confusion, because Uncle Levi sighed a little bit and started over.

"You have the very special and unique ability to lift the veil separating our two planes, but even your gift is somewhat limited because you cannot create view ports and see the past or more specifically, your past lifetimes as I can, so I will tell you your tremendous intellect has traveled with you through out each and every life you have lived. Do you remember the day you spelled 'nuclear physicist' at the nursery school?"

I nodded.

"Your affinity for nuclear physics, which you felt even as such a young girl, is a left over remnant from your previous lifetime when you and I were in fact two of the very first nuclear physicists in Europe."

"We were? Wow, that's really cool!"

He held up a hand to stop me from inquiring further. "However, each one of us in human form brings into each incarnation, something from previous lifetimes on the material plane *and* something learned on the ethereal plane. You, for example, in addition to your exceptional intelligence in each and every lifetime you have lived on the material plane have also had need to achieve, often to the detriment of personal relationships. But on the ethereal plane, you learned to develop and maintain relationships quite easily. At some point in each lifetime of material existence, you come to the conclusion that you need to develop and maintain relationships as well. Although that realization generally occurs later on in your life, it happens at an earlier age with each incarnation. That is something you should consider during this lifetime."

"You have also always had the tremendous gift to see people for who they truly are." He started on a new train of thought. "You don't look at outward appearances and often accept into your inner circle people that society would deem as less than desirable. I have always admired that about you. I actually believe it is this particular gift that has brought the Universal Energy to lift the veil of all existence for you. You will not be fooled by the intentions of others. You see, Jane, (his voice changed and he was suddenly cautious in his word choice) Zank Xu is one soul in particular you must be wary off. He is driven by power. As we accept the loving energy of each other in our family, he uses the energies of his family members to acquire more power. He forces them into allowing him to absorb their energy and uses fear of punishment to maintain his control. You must keep careful watch for him and for his family who will do his bidding if only to avoid his wrath."

"You mean there are bad people on the ethereal plane too? I thought we would all be safe and happy there. That's what they taught us in school. We would recognize each other as we remember them in this life but we would all be perfectly happy. Are they wrong?" I asked sincerely.

"Not exactly." He changed from his cautious conversational tone to what I called his 'teaching voice'. "Each religious group has its own explanation of what material plane inhabitants call the afterlife." Uncle Levi started speaking in what I now called his full blown 'lecture' mode. "In human form it is important to us to try and understand what happens when our physical life ends. You see what you are referring to is what we and you commonly call heaven."

"Wait. You're not from heaven? I thought that is where we are supposed to go when we leave this life." I was suddenly quite confused and I hoped the interruption would bring him back into conversational form.

"No," he said. "There really is no commonly accepted name for the ethereal plane, as I know it. Do you remember the classes you had that talked about purgatory? That may be the best description for the religious beliefs you are being raised with right now. Other belief systems think of it in other terms. But since this is your current understanding I will use it as the example."

"Yes," I said suddenly having an inkling of where he was going. "That's where we go to pay for the sins we committed during our time here on earth. After we have done our time there, then we get to go to heaven."

"You make it sound like jail!" Uncle Levi laughed at my analogy.

"Well, sure, that's how it seems to me," I said taking no offense at his laughter. I knew it wasn't mean-spirited. "You know, you do the crime; you do the time? Right?"

"Oh dear," said Levi, "this is going to require some explanation. Humans on the material plane have long been trying to make sense of what comes after their physical life. This is reasonable since we cannot accept that life merely ends with the death of the physical body and physics dictates that energy cannot be destroyed only altered. And of course it's appropriate, as you well know since you, from the material plane and I, from the ethereal plane, are even having this conversation. There is so much more to existence then even I can tell you. What you understand to be purgatory is simply another type of being. Yes, according to your understanding, I currently reside in what you might believe to be purgatory, but that is actually the ethereal plane. Our energies live many lifetimes so that we can grow and develop into that which pleases the Universal Energy. Once we achieve that level, we believe we are elevated to a higher plane of existence or what you and in fact we as well call heaven. We do not know exactly what heaven is since we have no contact with anyone who has reached that level. We do know that these are wonderful souls who have lived many, many lifetimes and have grown into wise, just, sympathetic, humble, reverent and respectful energies. We know that they have departed our plane of existence and have not been reborn to the material plane."

"I guess that makes sense to me." I nodded my understanding. "But it's all very scary at the same time. What is it that I am supposed to do with my ability to see and talk to you? I see only family members so how can I see this dark soul you were talking about if he is not part of our family? Why would he want to bother with me, anyway? I'm just a kid; I don't have any ability to help him gain any power. I don't have any power to take."

"We haven't figured all of it out yet, Jane, but we are diligently working on it. We are watching the world through the same mechanisms that I have used to teach your history lessons. We see everything, and as I have told you before, there are no time constraints for us. We see the past, present and future as we wish. Knowing who he is, we are trying to follow his family through history through the present and into the future to see what clues may be left that we might decipher his plans. We know he wants to gain control of both planes of existence. We just don't know how he plans to accomplish that goal as of yet."

"But again, I don't control anything." I was becoming defensive. "My circumstances are such that I am under the control of my parents who seem more focused on my sister and her needs than on mine."

"Oh, I don't know about that, Jane," said Uncle Levi realizing I had just shifted topics. "I think your parents see a lot more than you give them credit for."

"Really? Why don't they ever seem to do anything that would benefit me instead of her? If there is a choice to be made, they always, and I mean always, favor my sister Josie. Sometimes, I think they seem to do the opposite of what is best for me just to purposefully hold me back. It's like they want to be sure I stay in the very tiny box they think I should fit into at least in their minds. Either they don't have the ability to or they aren't willing to see me. They make choices about my future based on how it will affect Josie. Like when, my class all took the standard state placement exams. The school told Mom and Dad that I should be placed at least several grade levels ahead of where I am. They won't tell me how many grade levels, but you and I both know I don't need to be in grade school. Anyway, the school board was willing to let me skip ahead a few grade levels since that was the only remedy they could offer for my situation. My parents thought of my sister first. They thought how hurt she would be if I passed her up. It was more important to them to do what they thought was best for Josie than to do what was clearly best for me."

"You sound angry," Levi said with concern.

"I am angry. I don't understand why I don't count as much as she does? All along Mom has been so happy to have one child with academic gifts and so I try to please her and do really well in school and then I find out that she is the one who is holding me back. I don't get it at all. It's kind of like the Peanuts characters, Lucy and Charlie Brown. Lucy holds a football for Charlie Brown to kick. He trusts her to hold it and not to hurt him because she is supposed to have his best interests in mind. She is supposed to be his friend. But every time he goes to kick that ball she pulls it away and he lands flat on his back. That's what my parents have done to me. They tell me to work hard and do well in school. But when I do they pull the football away and say nope just kidding, your sister is more important than your happiness or success. It doesn't matter to them at all that I earned the opportunity to move ahead. I *earned* it and they decided that I didn't matter."

"Hmmm." Uncle Levi was thinking deeply about what I had said. "You have always had achievement as your most basic internal motivation. Everyone in your family has relationships as their motivation. Perhaps, your parents think it is more important to maintain the relationship between you and your sister than it is for you to jump ahead a few grades?"

I was upset now. I had expected Uncle Levi to be on my side. "How could that possibly be the right thing to do? They are purposefully holding me back so she can feel better about herself? Talk about a crushing injustice. It's not fair and it's not right."

"I am beginning to understand why you have been placed with this family. Clearly you need to learn to develop relationships early on during this lifetime. Yes, yes," he said, nodding his head and then pointing his pipe at me, "I believe this is most likely what you need to learn in this lifetime. Developing and maintaining relationships sometimes means doing what is best for the other person even when it seems painful to you. Yes, yes," he said still nodding his head, "now the picture begins to focus."

I protested. "But I have had relationships in other lifetimes. Look at you! You said you and I have had a strong relationship especially in our last lifetime."

"Yes, that is very true. But you and I are very much alike," he said. "It is easy for us to work well together. You need to be able to become empathetic with people you are not like. You need to be able to put yourself in their shoes, so to speak."

"I don't understand," I replied truthfully "What do you mean?"

"To put yourself in her shoes means that you must try to imagine yourself as Josie," Levi began. "How would you feel if your little sister passed you by? Now imagine yourself in your parent's place. You have one remarkably gifted child who has an incredible sense of self and is not dependent upon any material possession or appearance and then you have another child who is emotionally fragile and whose entire self image is truly based upon what she perceives to be her place. What would you do? You must choose between disappointing a child whom you know can handle the disappointment and crushing the fragile ego of the other child who may never recover from the blow. Which course of action do you choose?"

"Okay, I see your point. I don't like it, but I do see it."

Chapter XXII: Sir Orville

My family has many allies on the other side. These families are not "connected" to us through anything other than friendship but, as Gillius has often said, the bonds of friendship are strong and true. Sir Orville St. John is a true friend of the Quintus family. I believe that Gillius would trust Sir Orville with the safety of his soul and the souls of our family. In fact, that is exactly what he did. It was Sir Orville that Gillius went to see when he left the meeting with Lucille and Melvin at his home. He needed to enlist the insight and support of his old friend. Sir Orville was only too happy to help.

"There! I see him!" Decreed a teenaged stable boy standing atop a wall made of stone at the entrance of the drawbridge on the estate created by a noble family of the middle ages. "Look! Look! He's coming!"

Sir Orville St. John dressed in the attire of a medieval knight and carrying a shield with his family coat of arms emblazoned upon it, rode along with two other men, all were on horseback. The group followed behind his page who was riding a horse much more suitable to his size. The boy carried a flag with the same crest as Sir Orville's shield. They were tired and hungry when they finally emerged through the deep, deep forest green fog that skillfully obscured the St. John estate entrance.

"You are certain neither Zank Xu nor his henchmen are sniffing around?" Sir Orville inquired of the stable boy as they came into view from the fog and entered the clearing before the drawbridge.

"I searched all over before you deployed the fog and have been standing careful watch ever since, they is nowhere to be seen, Sir Orville!" The boy who had jumped down from the wall replied as he gathered the reins of the page's horse once the party entered the property.

Two men greeted the group at the entrance way as well. They were dressed in the garb of a stable man and a groundskeeper. They accepted the reins of the other horses from their riders who had stepped down from their steeds. They led the horses toward the stable to feed and care for them after their long trip.

The page accompanied his horse to the stable (he and the stable boy were clearly friends) while the three travelers made their way across the stone path inlaid in the ground to provide dry and safe access across the open grassy field between the stable and the large estate mansion.

SIR ORVILLE

"Come my friends," invited Sir Orville, "we will have supper and drinks and discuss the implications of the information gleaned upon our journey."

They entered the castle-like home and were followed by a cloud of dust from their cloaks. The Lady Nora greeted them in the hallway.

"Isn't it interesting," she began, "that even in this realm, you men still have the need to trail dirt and dust wherever you go!"

Laughing, Sir Orville jibed, "But of course my heart. Men do not feel like men unless a manly mess we make!"

"Well then, my husband, take your manly mess into the dining area and I will send in some sustenance." She winked and smiled as a servant took Sir Orville's and both guests' cloaks.

At a large wooden table in a medium sized dining room off of the grand hall (that was used for large family functions and entertaining on a much larger scale), Sir Orville and his two comrades sat to discuss the situation before them over food and drink provided by Lady Nora and the servants.

"You may be assured we will help you in any way we can offer Sir Orville. Together we have journeyed far and met with many, many other families all in your quest to gather information about the current activities of Zank Xu. However, we are concerned that knocking on doors, so to speak, and inquiring about the goings on of such a powerful energy will only draw attention. We must inquire, why are you putting your entire family in this tenuous position?" asked the larger and more hairy of the two companions.

"What I tell you now I must ask you to keep secret and to discuss it only between ourselves. May I count on your discretion?" Sir Orville asked. As his friends nodded silently, he continued, "We have offered refuge on our estate to *his* former first advisor, the single soul who can provide the Quintus family with the information they need to protect their newest arrival to the material plane from the influence of Zank Xu."

"This is disturbing news indeed!" Said the larger man. "But *why*? I must ask, why put your family and friends for that matter so directly in harm's way?"

Sir Orville was silent for a moment and smiled a bit as if he was remembering with nostalgia. "It is a huge debt we owe the Quintus family. One we may not be able to repay even over the course of eternity. It was truly a harsh time when the black plague struck us. Within only mere weeks our entire family passed to the ethereal plane. We were confused and unsure of what we were expected to do. How should we live? Where should we go? There were so many of us, adults and children, infants and animals. We were too innumerable for those in our family who had gone before us to welcome all at once. They tried to help, as many as was feasible as quickly as they could but the majority of us were lost and wandering. We could have fallen easy prey to Zank Xu. It was Gillius Quintus and Lucille who organized our family's energy and showed us how to protect ourselves from his probing and the attacks that he would send in an attempt to join his energy to our own. Even after all they have done for us they have never asked for, nor expected, anything in return from us. Truly, we owe them more than we can ever hope to repay. So, you see, when Gillius himself came to me and asked this favor, I could not say no. I would not say no. It is the very least we can do for the family that stayed with us, guided us, and showed us everything we needed. They taught us how to feed and clothe ourselves, and how to keep our family energy strong and intact. They even helped us design and build this castle and the estate we enjoy so immensely. This small favor sorely pales in comparison to the acts of kindness and protection they have given my entire family. We gladly join our energy to theirs and call them friends for eternity."

"I see," said the smaller, less hairy man. "I certainly understand the need to at least attempt to repay a debt...but to go against the likes of Zank Xu, who it seems to this point has ignored your presence, by hiding and protecting the one soul you know he seeks most...well, I must say you are decidedly braver than I, Sir Orville. You have cloaked the entrance to your family's energy home but how can you prevent intrusion of someone so powerful as he? Sooner or later, you know someone will speak and he will get the information he so desperately seeks. What will you do when Zank Xu comes for his former first advisor?"

"Gillius and I are diligently working on that dilemma." Sir Orville called to a nearby servant, "have the guards at the gate reinforce the energy barrier before the drawbridge and have them protect the rear entrance as well. We do not want any uninvited guests." And turning back to his friends he calmed them with, "May we count on your continued support in our patrols and inquiries?"

The two men looked to each other; and again the larger, hairier man spoke. "Aye! That you may; we will lend any and all aid it is within us to provide."

"I thank you for that." Sir Orville offered sincere gratitude. "For now, let us just enjoy ourselves. Anything you gentleman want or need please ask or feel free to create it as you see fit. Joyful energy abounds in my family home and I gladly share it with you, my friends. I am most grateful for your company and your aid and intend to extend every courtesy and comfort. Eat! Drink! My wife is very proud of the pudding before you." Sir Orville clapped his hands together twice and demanded, "Music!"

Chapter XXIII: Jane Meets The Council

Things had changed a bit around the La Roi homestead. My sister Josie and I each had our own rooms now. Our parents had grown tired of our fighting every night. Since Joaney went away to college, her room had become a sewing area, but Mom and Dad decided that peace in the family was more important. I moved into Joaney's old room and Josie got our room all to herself. Joaney's room was smaller so Josie was happy she came out on top. I was just so glad the nightly torture and teasing was over, at least for the most part.

I was fast asleep one night when Uncle Levi came to me in a dream. He had never done that before, but I was happy to see him any way.

He sat down on the bed next to me and very gently he said, "Listen Jane, I know we were going to introduce you to each member individually, but circumstances have changed. It is important for you to meet the Family Council now. You may remain asleep, your rest is also important. I will help you cross the veil to the ethereal plane and we will visit the council chamber together."

With that he held out his hand and I reached up automatically and took hold of it. At least, I thought I got up to walk with him.

The sensation is difficult to explain, but I noticed right away that I was lighter and did not feel my feet on the cold linoleum bedroom floor. When I looked back at my bed and realized I was still lying there sound asleep.

"This is weird." I said a bit nervously, "but kind of fun and exciting too."

"This is a big moment for all of us Jane. It is important that you be very respectful of the family elders. Be on your best behavior, understand?"

"Sure, okay. I promise."

We entered the purple haze and I saw the brilliant emerald green light that always appeared with Uncle Levi, but this time there was a smaller golden light playing in the haze as well. "Funny," I thought, "I've never noticed that color light before."

"That color you see is you, Jane. It is how your energy appears on the ethereal plane. That colorful light is one of the ways that others you have known in your many lifetimes recognize your energy by."

We approached what looked to be a really dark long hallway at the end I could see some activity in some sort of room but I couldn't say I could recognize or identify anything. All of a sudden, we were at the end of that long hallway and standing in large open room with windows on one side and portraits hanging on two others and a giant, I guess I would call it a family crest on the last wall. There was a really large lavishly carved wooden table in the center of the room with the people I had first met the day I arrived with the adoption worker all sitting around it.

There was the man with gray hair still wearing what I thought was a sheet so long ago, and the lady with the high collared dress and the beautiful cane at her side on opposite ends of the table. It's funny, both of their colors were sort of shimmering metallic. Hers was bright sparkling silver and his was more like mom's platinum wedding ring set. It was almost polished and honed. Both were really quite beautiful to me.

There was the lady in the sparkly dress with the feather in her headband. She was an incredible red-orange. Wow, was her energy bright! The marine was a vibrant azure blue and the lady dressed in the clothing of the American west was sort of a robin's egg blue. It's a good thing I had a box of sixty-four colors at home or I probably wouldn't have made the differences between them. The man who was clearly an early American settler had a burnt orange, or maybe it was copper, energy. Yes, copper definitely. It was also quite striking and lovely. I could have just stood there and watched the pretty light show; at least that's how I thought of it. Each member of the council was surrounded by his or her color. It was then; I realized the room was suddenly bright and inviting. I felt warm and safe. I really liked it there.

"Perhaps you should begin, Lucille?" said the man in the sheet.

"Of course," she replied as she stood at her seat. "Welcome, Jane! Welcome!" she said with affectionate enthusiasm. "We are so pleased you are here. We have been watching your development throughout your life and we are so very delighted with your progress. I cannot find the words to express how grateful we are to the Universal Energy for your ability to visit us here."

I was a bit taken aback. She was acting like I was really something special and I didn't feel special at all. It's not like I had anything to do with acquiring my "gift". It's just always been there. I didn't earn it or anything.

"Oh but you are special, dear child," she continued. "You most certainly are a blessing to this family."

"Ok, now this is getting scary," I thought.

"Please, don't be frightened," came from the deep baritone voice at the other end of the table. "I can see you are a bit overwhelmed with our greeting and our appearance. Please everyone, reign in your auras a bit so we don't intimidate our little Jane."

With that command, the energy of everyone at the table became a bit more muted. That was pretty cool to watch. I understood that they were trying to put me at ease, so I allowed myself to relax a bit.

"How about a chair, Miss Jane?" the marine offered as he stood and held out a high-backed chair that wasn't there a second ago. I sat between the marine and Uncle Levi. The table was so high that my chin was right on top of it.

Uncle Levi laughed and said, "Let me help you with that."

Either the chair got taller or the table became shorter but suddenly, I was sitting at an appropriate and comfortable height to the table.

"Now this is what we have needed to even out this table and this council," the American West woman observed. "Two men and a woman on one side," she said as she smiled and nodded at me, "two women and one man on the other side, and one man and one women at each end. We are perfectly balanced with you here, Jane. How wonderful!"

"But," I thought, "I'm just a girl, not a woman."

"Oh dear, hasn't Levi explained that time does not matter here?" inquired the Victorian lady.

"Well yes, but..." I began.

"You see Jane," she continued, "your energy is the second oldest. We can say that because your first incarnation was during the early Renaissance period in Europe. In this group, only Gillius has been around longer, as you can see by the Roman Toga he wears."

"Gillius?" I managed to speak out loud this time; at least I think I did.

"Oh my, yes! Where are our manners?" the Victorian lady said with a small amount of dismay. "Jane, please allow me to introduce your family council to you. At the opposite end sitting at the head of our table is Gillius. To his left the gentleman who so thoughtfully gave you a chair is Melvin. Of course you know Levi; my name is Lucille. To my left is Louise and next to her is Jacob. Finally to Jacob's left is Caroline. We are the family council, or the family elders, if you will. We gather to make family decisions and to lead all those connected to us on this plane of existence."

"We have wasted too much of Jane's time, I am afraid," said Uncle Levi. "If you notice the time that has passed on the material plane, dawn is about to break. We need to get her back to her bed so she can wake up as usual."

"But I thought time doesn't matter here," I brought up.

"To us it doth not, but to you my dear, as your physical body is asleep in your room, it does," Jacob replied.

"Let us provide the information before it is too late," prompted Gillius.

Uncle Levi now turned to me and said, "Jane, you are becoming a young lady and it is no longer appropriate for me to just walk into your room whenever I choose. It must now be your choice to invite me in so that you have the ability to maintain some privacy."

Caroline spoke next. "We believe we have come up with a way for you to contact us when you need to Jane. We have put together our power of thought and made it into a rhyme so you may remember it even if you are scared. All you need to do is focus in your mind's eye on the path you took here with Levi and think with all your might these words:

I connect with thought of mind;
To ethereal beings beyond space and time
I seek knowledge and wisdom
Through the energy that binds.
I call to ancestors of the Quintus line.
Cross the veil and near me dwell.

"And then you just ask for which of us you want or whatever it is you need like this, if you need to talk to me say, From Caroline I need guidance, advice, and insight as well."

"Can you remember that darlin'? It is pretty catchy, ain't it?" Melvin was clearly pleased with their poem.

Jacob said, "Maybe thou shouldst repeat it back to us that we may be certain of its anchor in your mind."

"Sure," I said, "it's easy. If I need to talk to anyone here, even Uncle Levi, I should focus on the purple hazy swirls and say, 'I connect with thought of mind, to ethereal beings beyond space and time, I seek knowledge and wisdom through the energy that binds. I call to ancestors of the Quintus line. Cross the veil and near me dwell, From Uncle Levi I need guidance, advice and insight as well'."

"Very well done, Precious!" Louise praised and clapped her hands in excitement. "Remember you may call any of us, not only Levi. Some of us are just dying for a chance to help out."

Uncle Levi stood, "You must go back now, Jane."

He took my hand as I stood next to him. I waved goodbye to everyone else in the room. I was so happy to have met them, and so joyful that I would get to call on them when I needed too. I knew I would never feel alone again. But I realized things in my daily life were definitely about to change. "So I won't be seeing you every day then?" I asked.

"I will come when you call Jane, have no doubt of that. But I will only come when you call."

"But what if I need you and I can't call?"

"You have no worries there, my dear. Someone from the council will always be watching you for safety. We just will not interfere unless you ask us to, except if there is a dire need, of course."

We were standing next to my bed now where I still lay sound asleep.

"Get back into bed now, you have to get up very soon."

"Good night, Uncle Levi. Thank you! That was wonderfully remarkable!"

"Good night." And he walked back into the purple haze. "Oh," he said as he turned back toward me, "you should be careful not to 'remark' of tonight's activities to any one." He smiled and winked. I watched his green light disappear into the swirls of mist and then the haze closed in on it self. It sort of looked like when the water goes down in the toilet. "That's not a very nice description," was the last thought I had until Mom (I had finally started to call her 'Mom') rang that handbell she loved so much to wake us up. Gosh, I really hated that bell.

Section IV: A Prelude To War

On the ethereal plane, Zank Xu was positioning himself to gain the level of control he so desperately desired. The depths of evil that he was willing to exploit in his quest astonished everyone. While the Council was preparing for the conflict with Xu they all seemed to know was coming, I had a few battles of my own to wage. Some of life's most important lessons are learned through controversy, and some of the most surprising results arise because of it. The remainder of my fourth grade year was full of both lessons and surprising results.

Chapter XXIV: Zank Xu Steps Onto The Material Plane

Idiots! Fools!" Zank Xu raged at his advisors. "How is it that you three imbeciles are the best I have to choose from in my family? I cannot possibly be related to such inept and cowardly energies! Clearly something is wrong with the universe!"

The three advisors had returned from their discovery of the energy barrier of Sir Orville St. John's family estate and disclosed the information they gained during their reconnaissance.

Pacing and gesturing wildly, Zank Xu continued. "You know where the former first is hiding but you cannot get to him? Imbeciles! Morons! Worthless, the lot of you!"

"We thought it most prudent Master," began the new first, "to come to you with our discovery, rather than to alert the St. John family to our knowledge of their existence. Our combined strength is pitiful and not likely enough to breech the barrier they have constructed in order to hide their home from your greatness. If we attempted to gain access and failed they would likely increase its potency making it more difficult for your excellence to penetrate. We did not wish to tax your strength, great Master."

"Hmmmm. It is just possible that you are not quite a fool after all." Xu had stopped pacing and was thoughtfully rubbing the side of his chin with a long bony finger. Suddenly he turned to face his advisors. "But you are still all imbeciles! However, I will take your delayed action as a sign that you are capable of a small amount of logical thought...a very small amount."

"Oh thank you so kindly, exalted Master, of such high praise, we are truly unworthy." The new first bowed repetitively and backed up appropriately as Zank Xu strode back toward his throne.

He paused for a brief moment as if a thought has suddenly occurred to him and he raised an eyebrow. He began stroking his braided beard as he again paced the length of the platform on which his throne was elevated (of course). He stopped suddenly again and dramatically waved his arm to create a viewer into the material plane. "Show me the locations of the descendents of the Quintus line." Immediately the European and North American continents came into view. "Now, I wish to see the location of any new arrivals of the Quintus line." The United States came into focus. "I need a more specific geographic location than that!" He angrily fumed at the view port he had established.

With his venomous words the view port changed to show only his own image and then slammed closed. "What?" said a shocked Zank Xu. "Open! Open, I command!" And he waved his arms in grand violent sweeping movements, but the view port did not open. "What is this? Something is blocking me from seeing what I wish!" He halted abruptly as he saw Gillius in his mind's eye. "Gillius Quintus! I should have known it must be you! I have left your family alone long enough because I respected your strength. Now it is time for you to recognize mine! If I cannot find this child from the ethereal plane, I will do so from the material one." He said aloud as he purposefully and quickly stomped back to his throne. "Leave me!" he said to his advisors. "Do not return until you are summoned."

"Yes, Master. Yes, Master. As you wish, Master," the three advisors repeated over and over as they bowed just as repetitively until they exited the room.

Zank Xu thought about the tragedies he had suffered during his mortal life. He recalled that moment when he swore upon his immortal soul that he would gain back the importance and control he so desperately desired and certainly deserved. He remembered that he did make some small steps toward his goal while he still lived in the physical world. After the death of his wife, he wandered the mountains without any real purpose but it gave him time to contemplate all that had befallen him. He began to resent his father and he hated the Governor and everything that had been done to him. By the time he spied a small village in the distance, he had come to the conclusion, that none of what had transpired was in any way his fault. Of course, he had no responsibility for the deaths of any one of his family members. If only his father had told him of the payments to the Governor things might have been different. But Zank could not truly hate his father; he realized that in the old man's place he probably would have done the same.

Appearances and perception are reality, after all. If his father taught him anything, he taught him that. It was at that moment that Zank Xu had struck upon a wonderful idea. He had watched the villagers' comings and goings long enough to realize that they would not attack a starving and injured man. He made himself appear to be worse off than he was and wandered into the village. He told them he had been thrown from his horse and was searching the mountain for the animal. The villagers were kind and gentle people who took him in at once. While he lived there he quickly became the master broker he had previously been. When he saw that one villager had two pairs of socks and another had none, he guilted the citizen with two pairs into giving the one pair away for the good of his soul, and of course Zank Xu would generously hold them until he found someone in need. Then he went to the villager who had no socks but did have two chickens and convinced him that he would certainly die of a horrible disease that he would contract through the soles of his feet if he did not wear socks. It was then a simple matter to trade the villager the socks for a chicken. He now had eggs to bargain with as well. He continued to grow his business and even convinced the villagers to confer upon him the title of Master Trader. They made him responsible for all commerce of the entire village. He expanded his power base from deals within the confines of the entire village and extended it to negotiations with a neighboring village on another mountain ridge. Of course, each transaction provided him with some form of remuneration. It was only fair, after all.

If he had been given enough time in the mortal realm, Zank Xu was quite certain, he would have controlled all commerce in the mountain area and maybe even all commerce in the province. If only he had been given the time, he would certainly have put that Governor in his place. Unfortunately that was not to be. A trader came to the village carrying not only wares for barter but also a deadly fever. Zank Xu contracted the fever and died within days.

"It's funny," he thought, "how all of these memories came rushing back. It must be that the energy of the Abyss is trying to tell me something." He had been contemplating the deal struck between his father and the Governor that had cost his family their lives when he first came upon the notion of a trade with the energy of the Abyss. So far, their exchanges had been quite satisfactory. He settled into his chair, placed two bony fingers to his temple and his thumb to his jaw and closed his eyes. He entered a deep trance. He saw the Abyss in the distance and called to it. "I call beyond the ethereal realm to the being of the Abyss that has helped me before. Increase the power of my energy so I may possess a mortal on the physical plane. I give you one family member as payment." And then almost as an afterthought he added, "Oh, but not my advisors, if you please, they are morons but they do my bidding as best they can."

Just as asked, the energy of one family member was extracted from its hovel of a home and sucked into the Abyss from which as yet no energy has ever returned.

As he watched the terror of the soul being pulled into the Abyss, he chuckled to himself. "An excellent choice, that one was truly good and clearly bound for higher elevation following his next incarnation. He might have caused me trouble after another lifetime and should provide me with greater strength than the others taken before."

Zank Xu felt his strength and power begin to rise. He felt the swelling of greatness within himself. "I *am* the most powerful being on this or the material plane. There is no one greater than I." He laughed a cold, evil laugh.

"Now, down to business. I must find someone of value to direct." He sat back deeply in the throne and mentally searched the material plane for a descendent to control. "Why, of course," he said as the father of Po Duk Xu came into focus. With that thought, he created the swirling, black, smoky mist he used to enter the material plane. Black beams of anti-light that shined with a metallic reflection followed him as his energy entered the vortex. He found himself standing in the home of Samlin Xu. "Now, where is that weak fool?" Just as he finished the thought, Samlin (or Sam as he preferred) came around the corner and saw Zank Xu standing there. He was startled by the presence of someone uninvited and dressed so oddly in his home. As he was briefly in shock, his mind was empty for just a moment; (that was why Zank Xu had shown himself). It was at that instant he stepped into Sam Xu and took over his body and mind. Sam's energy was still intact. It was being held hostage, tied up securely by the power of the energy of Zank Xu. As much as he tried, Sam could not move or control his body. It was like he had been tied to a chair, gagged and shoved away in a closet at the end of a long dark hallway. He was still there but he was definitely not in charge.

"At last," said Zank Xu as he examined Sam's hand and arm and controlled the movement of the fingers. "I do not merely speak to the mind of this one or just impart ideas to that one; I have complete control of mind and body. Shut up!" he said to the struggling Sam in his head. "I will give you back your body soon enough. I only need to borrow it for a while." He turned to leave the residence and found himself standing directly in front of Po Duk, who had witnessed the entire event.

Chapter XXV: Cooperation or Disgrace?

Zank Xu was now in control of Sam's body and he used it to do as he pleased. He controlled the corporation of which Sam was the owner and Chief Executive Officer and had minions to physically carry out his wishes. Zank Xu was living the high life on the material plane and greedily laughed to himself in his plush comfortable chair, staring out the large window of his high-rise office while his manicurist polished his nails. He recalled the recent occurrence when he set eyes on Po Duk, as he possessed the boy's father's body. He was actually quite pleased that Po Duk recognized immediately that he controlled his father's body.

"All those hours I spent reaching into that useless woman's belly to forge a bond with this child have actually paid off. He knows who I am *and* will do my bidding if for no other reason than to save his father. He has felt my power from the womb. He knows there will be no mercy for his father should I be disappointed. Indeed all of my effort was exhausting but it truly was energy well spent and bargains well struck with the being of the Abyss." Zank Xu was very proud of himself. He pushed a button on an intercom and screamed into it.

"Foolish and insignificant woman, report at once to my presence!" Immediately, a secretary entered the office. Zank dismissed the manicurist with a wave of his hand saying, "You may leave now." He turned to the secretary in front of him. "Put every available member of this pathetic company on this single task. I want to know the location of every child born on the same day as my son on the North American continent."

"But, sir," the secretary began, "such an enormous undertaking will take many people away from their current functions."

"*You are fired! Get out! Get out!*" screamed an irate Zank Xu. He quickly moved into the outer office. "Is there anyone here competent enough to carry out my wishes?"

"I will do as you ask, sir," came a timid voice from the first desk to his left. "Aha," said Zank, "I have a new first. There is always someone willing to serve the power to embolden their own position."

"Excuse me, sir?" The woman timidly inquired. "I apologize but I do not understand your meaning."

"You have no need to understand, you simply need to act. Now do as I have commanded. Use every computer device and every person necessary to obtain the results I demand!"

"Of course, Mr. Xu, right away sir." The secretary, or the material first as Zank liked to think of her, hurried away on her mission. "Hmm, I must consider utilizing females on the ethereal plane. At least they are more pleasant to look upon while they are being incompetent." He returned to Sam's office and closed the door. He slowly walked over to the couch and stretched out. "Alas, I am becoming weaker. I must get this family to the North American continent. I do not know if I can maintain my presence here long enough to ensure this will happen." With that thought he looked inward to the still struggling Sam Xu.

want your body back?" Zank spoke slowly and deliberately His voice had an evil seductive tone to it. [It was really ghtening.]

Sam nodded furiously.

"Good. Then you will do as I say or, make no mistake, I will step right back in and find a way to disgrace you and your family. Perhaps I will even take that foolish woman you live with back to the ethereal plane with me. Do you understand?"

Sam nodded again, but slowly this time.

"You will complete the task I have assigned your office staff. When you have found the child born the same day as your son with ties to the Quintus line, you will move your family there. Success is the only acceptable outcome."

Sam stared back at him.

"Don't look so suspicious." Zank decided he should impart a small amount of information to Sam. "Yes, I have a master plan of course. Your boy will marry this girl thereby joining our two families for eternity. I will become the most powerful ethereal being and that bothersome Quintus family will be under my control. You will, of course, be granted the prestigious position of becoming my advisor when your time on the material plane is complete."

Again, Sam stared.

"Do you understand, you fool?" Zank roared. "It is customary and usual to nod if you grasp the severity of your situation!"

Sam nodded very slowly.

"What is it to be then, cooperation or disgrace?"

Sam hung his head for a moment. Then he raised it, looked directly at Zank Xu and nodded again.

"Excellent!" Zank Xu said with knowing glee. He felt troubled for only a moment but he just could not pinpoint the problem, and then he realized he was losing the power to maintain his possession of Sam. "No! Not now! Not yet!" He thought to himself with the sudden realization that he was becoming significantly weaker; the energy boost from the Abyss was wearing off. He needed to quickly return to the ethereal plane. Before doing so, Zank Xu screamed into the intercom one more time.

"Have my son brought to my office this instant!"

When the child arrived, Zank Xu placed both hands on the boy's head. There was a surly quality of tone in his voice. "Pay attention, boy." Zank Xu allowed Po Duk to see into his mind. He saw his father frightened, tied up and gagged. Zank Xu tortured the cowering soul of Sam Xu with the same swirling black mist that caused the agonizing pain, choking and gasping of the former first and he forced Po Duk to watch. He was sure he controlled both of them now.

As he was about to depart from Sam and the material plane, he said to Po Duk, "I know you understand, boy. In case he gets brave, make certain you remind your father of what is in his best interests... and yours."

Po Duk smiled and nodded, his face took on an evil gleam if for only a moment.

With that, Zank Xu stepped out of Sam Xu's body and entered the black swirling mists to return to the ethereal plane. Sam Xu loudly sucked in a deep breath as if he hadn't taken in any air in a very long time. He sat up and looked with fear and uncertainty at his son who only stared back at him.

Chapter XXVI: The Incident with Creepy Moe

As was the fear of the family Council, Zank Xu had brought the fight to the material plane. They were busy pushing ahead with their plans to somehow fend him off. They hadn't yet discussed with me how they intended to defeat Xu, but I really wasn't all that concerned about it any way. I had much greater (as far as I was concerned) and more immediate issues to deal with.

I was sitting next to one of my two school friends on the bus ride home one day early on in my fourth grade year. We were talking about the upcoming tryouts for the class Christmas play even though Christmas was still more than two months away when, all of a sudden, a huge spit wad (that's paper soaked in spittle, for those with a classier upbringing) came across the aisle and hit me squarely on side of the face. There was a moment of what seemed like total silence and then the whole section across the way from me that was occupied by fifth graders, erupted in an uproar. I was totally taken by surprise. I was absolutely shocked. I even froze for a moment because I didn't know what to do. Speechless, I looked across the aisle for the culprit or an explanation. There he was...Moe Plakkot (Plack Oh). Moe was the biggest, meanest and dumbest boy in the fifth grade. He had a huge mole just to the right of the center of his forehead. Thinking back, I don't really know what I wanted to do but the incident was so shocking and so gross that I actually screamed. It was a deep guttural, blood – curdling scream.

"Hey, Jane! Ya got something on your face there!" said a smarmy Moe. And then the laughter started again. I felt that familiar sinking deep down in the pit of my stomach and I felt the anguish starting to rise up from my toes. I was going to burst into tears and I knew it. I remember that I desperately did not want to cry in front of the other kids. I knew that would cause me unspeakable torture for the rest of the year, but I also knew I couldn't stop it.

And then I got the next biggest shock of my young life. To me, at least, this was even bigger than when Uncle Levi took me to meet the Council. My sister Josie, who was now a fifth grader, saw the entire incident. She saw that I was going to cry and she didn't hesitate. She was up and out of her seat and throwing punches at the biggest, meanest boy in her class. Watching her in action was such a surprise; I actually forgot that I wanted to cry. Josie never hit anyone but me. She was always so sickeningly sweet she would bat her eyes and get her way and yet, there she was yelling and cursing and pummeling the snot out of Moe Plakkot. No really, she knocked a huge gooey booger right out of his nose.

"That's my sister, you ★&%##&★%★ creep!" she screamed.

I don't think I should repeat the expletives I have deleted from her rant, but you must certainly get the idea that my sister was really angry. I would say she was even enraged. Moe never had a chance.

The bus driver, who had been watching through the mirror, pulled the bus over unbuckled his seat belt and stood up. That was never a good sign. He picked up his clipboard and yelled, "Everyone settle down and take your seats." He trudged down the aisle and stopped right at creepy Moe and stared down at him. There was either a slight look of hatred or amusement in his eyes. I couldn't tell which, really. I thought he might have changed from one to the other. Then, he took the pen from his shirt pocket and wrote out the dreaded "white slip". That was the report from the driver that you got if you misbehaved on the bus. You had to give it to a parent and have them sign it and return it to the driver before you were allowed to ride the bus again. He handed one white slip to creepy Moe, at which I admit I smiled. But he also gave one to Josie, and that wasn't so funny.

Josie protested of course. She looked the really large man right in the eye. "I was defending my little sister!"

He looked over at me for a moment. "Your sister looks like she can defend herself," he said as he turned and walked back to the front of the bus to continue the trek home.

Josie looked at me, the anger was still vibrantly obvious in her eyes; she shook her head and turned away with a huff.

When we reached our driveway, we got off of the bus. We were walking that long, stone-filled pathway to the house when I said, "Thanks for beating on him for me." I paused for just a second before I asked, "Why did you do that?"

"Because you're my sister, moron!" Josie said with exasperation. "The driver is right, you know, you could defend yourself if you wanted to. Even I get tired of seeing you picked on all the time; why don't you stand up for yourself once in a while?"

"I don't know. I never thought of it I guess," I said sort of sheepishly.

"And *you're* supposed to be the smart one!" she said as we got to the door.

We entered the breezeway or mud room of our home; we left our jackets and shoes, and found Mom standing at the top of the few stairs that lead to the kitchen.

"How was your day, girls?" she always said with a bright tone and a smile.

"It's not my fault; it's hers," grumbled Josie as she handed the white slip to Mom and stomped into the kitchen.

That night alone in my room, I thought about what she said. My conversation with myself went like this: "I probably should stand up for myself shouldn't I? Maybe I should ask someone. Josie isn't always the most reliable source of helpful information. I want to ask a woman though. I love Uncle Levi but he has no idea what it's like to be a girl. The Council did say I could call on any of the other members and I would like to talk to Louise, maybe I will try to call just for her."

I closed my eyes and pictured the purple haze I had seen whenever I was in the presence of an ethereal family member. I tried really hard to focus on that purple haze and thought I saw Louise on the other side of it. I repeated the rhyme the Council had given me to call to them when I needed too.

"I connect with thought of mind,
To ethereal beings beyond space and time.
I seek knowledge and help
Through the energy that binds,
I call to ancestors of the Quintus line.
Cross the veil and near me dwell,
From Louise I need guidance, advice, and wisdom
as well."

Louise came through with a brilliant red-orange beam of light. She also had someone I hadn't met in chambers with her. This person was a woman too; she was a bit heavy set and had short bobbed hair. She was dressed in jeans and a tee shirt that read "E.R.A. Now!" There was a pale light with her. I guess I would have to call it fuchsia or maybe a magenta colored light.

"Hello, precious," said Louise. "I was so hoping you would call for me. I know you want some help standing up for yourself. We girls have got to stick together you know. I brought my friend Dina with me. Dina is really great at standing up to opposition. She spent her last two lives trying to make equal rights for women into law. She was a Suffragette when we lived together on the material plane and most recently she lived during the 1960s and early seventies when women made some really great strides in equality much of it thanks to her efforts."

"Hello," I said to Dina.

"Hey kid!" she said back. "What's your question?"

"Well," I began, "my sister says I should stand up for myself when someone does something mean to me or something isn't fair. Should I? Or, is it best just to let it go and avoid a confrontation?"

"Of course you should take a stand!" said Dina. "You can't let other people run you over just because you're little or because you are a girl. That's just not right. You need to get in there and fight not just for yourself but to protect all the other little girls who are going to be in the same boat as you some day. See, kid, I wasn't fighting the government and society only for my rights, but for my daughters and her daughters too. In fact, I fought for all daughters and all future generations of women on the material plane. We cannot let ourselves be held down by men or by unfair laws or societal judgments. It's our choice to accept their rules of behavior or to stand up and do what's right for us by fighting back."

"But I don't really want to fight anybody. My sister just did that. It looks like it hurt and she got into trouble."

Dina laughed raucously. "Oh kid, you don't fight by physically punching someone. To make any real change you have to let your opinion be known. If something isn't right, you stand up and say so; and you do it loudly, so that everyone can hear you. After you make your point, you turn your back and walk out. Don't give your opponent an upper hand by letting them respond. Just turn and leave with your words hanging in the air like daggers falling from heaven."

"Really? Well, I can certainly do that," I said, starting to feel my emotions steeling inside me. I can stand up for myself like that for sure. "Thanks so much! I really appreciate your help! Thank you so much Louise for bringing Dina with you! You are both wonderful!"

"No worries precious! I help where I can, and when I can't I'll bring help with me. Call on me whenever you want to, even if you just want to chat. I'm looking forward to it!" Louise said as the purple haze began to engulf both her and Dina.

"Wait!" I suddenly said, loudly. Louise stepped back through. "I have another question I just thought of."

"Fabulous!" Louise said with joy.

"When I visited in the Council room, everyone's energy color, or aura as Gillius called it, was so vibrant and bright. Why are Dina's energy light beams so pale compared to everyone else's I have seen?"

"Oh that's easy, precious." Louise smiled and seemed to adjust her headband feather ("Did it get messed up from stepping back through the haze?" I wondered. A question for another time I decided.) "Dina is a new soul. She has only lived the two lifetimes I told you about. Our colors get brighter and stronger with each lifetime we live.

I needed to ask another question. "But my energy seemed light compared to everyone else's and you said my energy was the second oldest in the room. Why wasn't it more intense?"

"Easier still", said Louise, "Only part of your energy came to visit us in the Council room. Most of it was still asleep in your room. Bye for now, precious!" She stepped back into the purple swirls and they closed in after her.

I felt much better about everything. I was sure I could do what they had said. I smiled to myself and my mind was calm and peaceful. I thanked God in my prayers that I had Louise and Dina and the entire Council to help me...I thought it before when Uncle Levi returned with me from the Council chamber but now I had the sudden and true realization that I wasn't alone and had help whenever I needed it. I only had to call for it. That was really comforting and I knew my life would be different and better from that moment on. I drifted off to sleep. The best sleep ever.

Chapter XXVII: Gillius And Sir Orville

Louise and Dina had helped me become strong enough to stand up for myself and for what I believed in. I thought it was interesting that Gillius and Sir Orville had a similar problem to contend with while guarding the former first advisor. Gillius arrived at the St. John estate to finalize their plan to defeat Zank Xu.

"Good day to you, young sir!" called Gillius from outside the stone entrance to Sir Orville's family manor.

"Good day to you sir," the young man atop the wall called back. "How did you find us? I thought the gateway was obscured by an energy field."

"For some it is," Gillius replied, but for friends of Sir Orville the entrance is open and clear."

"You must be a friend then," said the boy as he jumped down from the wall.

"That I am," Gillius returned warmly.

The young watchman asked, "May I announce your presence, sir?"

"You may. Gillius Quintus, to see Sir Orville."

The young man made a mad dash for the back of the property. A few short moments later he was back.

"Sir Orville requests you join him on the archery range. May I show you the way?"

"I thank you, young man, but I am familiar." Gillius smiled knowingly at him.

"As you wish, sir." The young man ran off to the stable area and Gillius moved toward the archery range. He left a blazing trail of platinum beams behind as he disappeared from sight.

Sir Orville was taking aim at a target a seemingly impossible distance away. His brother, Lord Bernum was joking and having a good time. "You'll never make that shot brother. I am willing to bet my quiver you'll miss by two lengths."

"I'll take that bet," said Sir Orville. "Get ready to turn over your entire quiver."

Just as he was about to release the arrow, Gillius appeared with a loud booming greeting.

"Hail, hail my friends!"

Sir Orville jumped at the sound and lost control of the arrow he was aiming. It fell unceremoniously and plopped about ten feet in front of them.

"Well," said Sir Orville laughing, "it wasn't two lengths!"

"No" said Lord Bernum, in hysterics, "it certainly was not. I propose the bet should wait for another time." He slapped Sir Orville on the back and turned to greet Gillius.

"Hail to you, Gillius! Welcome to our home! You could not have come at a better time for Orville. He was about to lose an entire quiver!"

"You have certainly created a wonderful setting for your family, Orville. The bright sunshine and crystal blue sky and the greenness of your grass have made me quite envious. I will have to make some adjustments to my domain upon my return."

"I have made some modifications since you were last here, my friend. At least the changes to the outside are mine. The alterations to the interior are strictly those of Lady Nora. After Lucille showed her how to see the living quarters of the wealthy a century or so after we lived, Nora insisted upon some of those comforts for our home. I cannot say I blame her; I so enjoy our wonderful little castle, and we have you and your family to thank for it. Come inside! Look around! And then we can sit and discuss our situation."

As they walked from the archery range to the back entrance of the castle, Sir Orville became serious. "The former first has been giving Nora quite a difficult time."

"Oh, in what way?" inquired Gillius. "He seemed so innocuous."

"That is exactly the problem," laughed Sir Orville, who had only been pretending to be serious. "You know Nora cannot stand timidity of spirit, and the former first would be scared of his own shadow if he could still cast one." But now Sir Orville stopped being playful and truly became more somber. "I have been told that our common foe is searching the material plane diligently for your young lady. I am however uncertain as to how much success *he* may have already had."

"And how did you come by this information?" Gillius inquired. "The former first could not have provided it since I know you have kept him safe and securely locked in your castle."

"Oh, that he is. Secure indeed," Sir Orville assured Gillius. "The energy barrier has worked out quite nicely. It seems that Xu's new second advisor has a fondness for Louise's place. He has been able to send word through mutual acquaintances back to us. It's not quite an underground movement in the Xu clan but it is certainly a start."

Gillius nodded. "It would take significant effort to forge an underground movement in the house of Xu. To ensure her safety, I have obscured Jane from the ethereal plane as best as I am able. I have placed a reflective energy around her. It is as if she were surrounded by mirrors. Whenever anyone who is unaware of its presence attempts to view Jane or her location, the view port will only show his or her own reflection.

Sir Orville was suddenly overcome by a great belly laugh. "Oh, how I would have enjoyed being a fly on the wall when that happened for the first time!"

They entered the castle and were greeted by Sir Orville's wife, the Lady Nora.

"Hail to you, Gillius Quintus! " Lady Nora was energetic in her greeting. "It is so wonderful to see you and on such a glorious day! "

"Hail to you, Lady Nora! It is marvelous to see you again my dear." Gillius paused briefly to consider his words. "I hope I am not being too presumptive but I was so hoping for some of that delicious pudding you served during my last visit. I have never tasted anything quite like it and I so enjoyed its energy building and protection qualities. I felt like an Olympic athlete when I left."

"I am in the process of creating more this very moment. You are not the only one who enjoys that particular recipe," Nora said with some merriment. "Our guest is really quite fond of it too. Poor dear is so drained of energy he is eating like he has not seen nourishment since he crossed over."

Sir Orville patted his belly. "Well, if anyone can fatten him up, my love, it's you. Gillius and I have matters to discuss now, would you please bring your pudding to my office when it's ready?"

Smiling, Nora responded. "Of course, dear. Work hard and accomplish much!"

Chapter XXVIII: The Xu's Come to America

The energy of the former first advisor was getting stronger while he remained in the custody of the Lady Nora and Sir Orville St. John but he was still too frightened to offer any help with the coming fight. After his terrifying encounter with Zank Xu, Samlin Xu was feeling the same way. He was terrified he would fail to complete the task required of him and his wife would suffer the consequences. Sam used every resource he had to do as he had been directed. He called a meeting with the administrative heads of each department and division of his company and gathered them around a large oval table. Before him was a list of every child born on the North American continent on the same day as his son.

"I recognize the enormity of effort it has taken each of you and all of the personnel under your supervision to create this list." Sam said, "Know that I am most grateful. However, this list is of little value to me without the knowledge of which of these names is connected to the Quintus family line. Is there any progress along that investigation?"

"No, Mr. Xu. Unfortunately, not," came a voice from his right.

"Now what?" said Sam to himself. "How will I ever discover which child comes from the Quintus line?"

The administrator seated at the table continued."The only records of a Quintus family we can find are more legend than fact. We have found a family named Quintus that served as Roman statesmen before the Common Era but all actual records of this family were destroyed during the Great Fire of Rome in 64 CE. Through the intense diligence of the data mining section of my division, we have found documents, stories really, that allude to another Roman statesman named Quintus that may have lived just after 100 CE. Unfortunately, we cannot as of yet discern if 'Quintus' is this man's given name or family name. And quite frankly, sir, some of the acts attributed to this man do not seem realistic, especially when considered in conjunction with the time period in which he supposedly lived."

A spark of curiosity came across Sam's face. "I would be most grateful if you would explain your last statement." He sat up in his chair and provided the administrator with his undivided attention.

"It would seem that this Quintus person was the force behind the rebuilding of a forgotten section of the city of Rome. It appears that, after Rome burned, all but one section was rebuilt mostly using slave labor. However, a single sector may have been left as a reminder of the devastation. The families that had lived in that district were held up to ridicule as given no assistance of any kind. It was as if they were shunned as a sacrifice to the force that brought the destruction. After seeing their poverty and devastation from years of ignorance, this Quintus fellow decided that these people should suffer no longer and that the just course of action was to help rebuild their section of the city. Somehow, he organized citizens and statesmen to work together in the process. The fragments of documents that I have been shown tell the story of a great man who enabled all classes of Romans to work together. He encouraged men, women and children of all backgrounds to put aside their differences for the benefit of the rebuilding of this one section of the city. He proclaimed that it was imperative that all citizens should do the right thing for the right reason every time and that the right action would be the most moral. He convinced the citizenry of Rome not to subject those inhabitants of that designated unclean area to such dire circumstances. He proclaimed it was time to move forward from the old ways and created a new order.

We have also found other documents possibly linked to this person that convinced the Roman rulers of the day to open their homes and palaces in order to provide shelter for the homeless and created food banks to feed the hungry. It seems like he may have organized one of the first social welfare systems ever recorded. But again, these documents are linked by the smallest connection of the name Quintus. We do not know if any or all of this information is regarding the same individual named Quintus or even if this is the same person whose line you seek."

Sam was now thoroughly intrigued. "I wish you to trace the genealogy of this person. He or one of his descendents may very well be the start of the lineage I seek."

"We have anticipated your interest in this direction of inquiry and have already created, to the best of our ability, a 'tracer' tree showing those members that are likely related to this Quintus. We have been able to connect several families to the area of the United States commonly referred to as the Great Lakes. Unfortunately, we have run into a few unforeseen difficulties with the construction of this tracer tree." The administrator hung his head at his perceived failure.

"Difficulties? What are the difficulties? Please explain immediately!" Sam became anxious. He felt they were on the right path. He felt it in his soul.

"A great many of these families are farmers. The children are born at home and the only documentation of their birth is in the family bible or some other such record. The concern is that the birth records may not all be accurate. Also, there is another greater difficulty, sir." The administrator stopped.

"Go on! This greater difficulty is what?" Sam switched from anxiety to agitation.

"We have established that one woman connected to the Quintus line did enter a hospital on the day of your son's birth and she herself gave birth to a female child that same day. However..." The administrator stopped again as if frightened to continue.

"However, *what?!*" Sam pounded his fist on the table. "You will provide all information accurately and immediately. No further stalling!"

"However," the administrator timidly continued, "the child was made available for adoption and all records have been sealed."

"Then *unseal* them!" an utterly irate Sam Xu ordered.

"I am afraid that we cannot, sir. It is impossible for us to access these American records from our location." The administrator almost whimpered.

"Well, then, if I cannot access them from here, I will go to America and open them myself." Sam Xu was resolute. He knew he was on the right trail and he intended to follow it. Finding this American girl may be the only way to save his family and he would gladly sacrifice her to save his wife and son.

"Show me the location of the hospital to which the Quintus family member was admitted," Sam demanded.

Another member seated at the table retrieved an atlas from the corner of the meeting room. He placed it on the table in front of Sam and opened it to the pages dedicated to the Great Lakes region of North America. He found the very small city of Monroe, Michigan, near the Lake called Erie and pointed it out for all to see. "There! There it is, sir!" He was genuinely excited to have been of some use.

"Yes, I see. You may return to you seat," said Sam. "I must strategize my next move. Only the top officers are to remain; the rest of you, return to your duties."

With that command all but a few left the room. Sam studied the atlas a bit longer and then decreed, "Here," he pointed to the next larger city along the lake. "The city called Toledo. It is here that I shall expand my corporation. From this site, I will avail myself of the port system, look, there is railway and water access and even an airport nearby; Toledo is an ideal site for expansion. Also, I will still be within reasonable distance of the smaller city to the north where the birth records are kept. Yes, this is an excellent location indeed."

He turned to his top officers gave them each specific orders.

"You, purchase the land necessary to construct my newest factory."

Turning to another officer he said, "You, make inquiries of the educational system of this area. My son must have only the best teachers."

And to his executive assistant, he said, "You will work with my wife to purchase our new family home in the United States. It should be close to our factory but away from the riff raff if any live in the area. Mrs. Xu must be pleased, but so must I. Do you understand?"

The executive assistant, who incidentally was the secretary from the outer office who volunteered to help when Zank Xu was occupying Sam, nodded politely and said, "I will begin at once, sir."

CHAPTER XXIX: THE BATTLE LINES ARE DRAWN

Sam Xu was making plans to move his corporation and his family to America. He knew he was up against a dangerous and formidable force in Zank Xu. He was not the only one making plans to protect his family. My ethereal family and their friends were not letting any dust gather under them either. Everyone was very busy pitching in for the battle they all knew must come.

The women of the St. John family were busy in the castle kitchen preparing large batches of the energy pudding while he former first advisor was crying desperate sobs in the corner. "He's coming! I am doomed! We are all *doomed!*"

The Lady Nora was busily directing the action in the kitchen. She was in no mood for self-pity from anyone, but especially not from this soul who had been howling gloom and doom since his rescue by the soldiers of Sir Orville. "Quiet, you! We are in this predicament because of your family leader. I would think that a soul brave enough to slip out of the hovel, in which he was held captive and tortured, would be able to hold his wailing in check!" The former first sniffled and shook from fear. The Lady Nora continued, "You managed to keep your courage long enough to find your way to Louise's speakeasy and were smart enough to ask for the protection of the Quintus family. I know there must be some small kernel of fortitude in there somewhere. Instead of wringing your hands and bemoaning your circumstances, why don't you at the least try to do something about it!

"*Doomed! Doomed!*" The former first cried louder causing the Lady Nora to soften a bit.

"Look, ehhh…it occurs to me that I do not even know your name." Nora asked more gently. "You have only told us to call you the former first and frankly that doesn't mean a thing to me. What is your name?"

"My…my n-name?" stammered the former first. The question seemed to break his panic.

"Yes, of course, dear, your name, what did your parents call you when you were a child on the material plane?" Nora was really curious now.

"My…my parents? Yes," nodded the former first, "I remember my parents. They loved me so much! And I loved them too! I remember now," he said, as if the fog were suddenly lifting, "My parents called me Cong Ming. It means 'smart'. I tried very hard to live up to my name. They were very proud of my academic achievements. But Master called me Qiezi before I became his advisor. I know it sounds like cheesy but it means eggplant. He thought it terribly funny to call me eggplant. Master called each of us by the name he chose for us rather than by the one we were given. I had forgotten about that."

Lucille and Louise arrived in the kitchen area, dressed appropriately and ready to work alongside Lady Nora and her family. Nora suspended her conversation for a moment and greeted them with a smile and a nod to acknowledge their presence but then continued on with the former first while the other ladies and girls of the estate bustled around the room. Some cooked and stirred or poured large vats of pudding while others cleaned cookware for reuse or placed kindling under the giant pots on the hearth. Still others swept the floor or made great stacks of provisions for those who would be fighting on the front lines of the pending battle. Seeing the importance of the conversation, Lucille and Louise chose not to interrupt. Instead, they joined the others who sewed together the skins that would be filled by the men for use with the catapult.

"But I thought you are the 'former first'? Did you take 'first' as your name?" Lady Nora was now asking in earnest.

"Of course not," a now much calmer former first replied. "The Master determined he needed more than one 'advisor' but decided we did not actually deserve to have real names since in his eyes he elevated us above our family members to serve him. He said that was a true privilege and an honor. He wanted to be certain we never thought ourselves too important so he took away our names and gave us numbers instead."

"And did you find living in the palace of Zank Xu to be an honor Cong Ming?" The Lady Nora inquired.

Cong Ming hesitated briefly at the sound of his name. "Oh my goodness, no! It was absolutely terrifying. Every minute spent there at the Master's beck and call, never knowing when his temper would erupt. It was horrible!"

"Well, you are safe now with our family and we are pleased to help you out of your situation. But I must ask you to lend a hand while we prepare for your former Master's arrival." She handed him a broom, smiled pleasantly enough but with a look that told him there would be no more whining. As she turned to manage the kitchen's activities, she continued. "Now, we need to keep the floor clean all the way to the screens, if you please."

"The screens?" a perplexed Cong Ming repeated.

"Yes, of course, the screens. Oh, I'm sorry, I mean the area over there, the wooden partition that breaks the wall before you enter the outer hall. It protects the passage leading to the buttery and pantry of course." Cong Ming stood in stunned silence for a fleeting moment and then sighed and smiled while he swished the broom from side to side.

"Cong Ming. Cong Ming. My name is Cong Ming," he said to himself over and over again, as he worked from one side of the enormous table in the center of the room to the other moving toward the screens as requested. "Cong Ming."

The men and boys were also all quite busy in the black smithy making great kettles of energy sapping sleeping formula. There were multiple fires blazing and the kettles were all bubbling. A giant extremely well muscled sweaty blacksmith was overseeing four other men using the great fire pits to fashion weapons and the squires and pages who had each been tasked with the use of very long tongs to carefully soak each arrowhead and battle-axe and mace in it. Still other boys covered in protective gloves and aprons painted the front of the shields and filled large skins with the sapping solution (as they called it) and stitched them up tight to be used with the catapult.

"Careful not to touch it, boys, you will sleep immediately and not have any strength until it wears off or until the Lady Nora makes you some pudding," the blacksmith warned.

Two smaller boys per fire pit hung on the ends of giant bellows to open and close them so the fires would burn very hot.

"Zank Xu is desperate to find the former first," began Lord Bernum who had stopped to check on the progress of the smithy. "He will likely stop at nothing to find him. Let us be certain our weaponry will deter him from reaching the castle for as long as possible."

"But, Lord Bernum," a nervous Page inquired, "what happens when the barrier falls and he breaches the castle walls? What becomes of all of us?"

"We fight, boy! We fight with every last ion and photon of our energy! We fight!" No one had seen Sir Orville walk through the door. He was not yet wearing his full suit of armor. He handed over his shield, lance, axe and mace for application of the solution. "Let us be certain, Bernum, that the archers are well armed and positioned."

"That they will be, brother. You may count on it!" Bernum turned to the squadron of squires. "Make certain the portcullis and postern gates are prepared with sapping solution as well lads. We wouldn't want anyone to cross with too much energy, now would we?" He laughed a great bawdy laugh as several boys gathered the supplies to paint the front and rear gates of the manor.

Chapter XXX: The Educational Testing System

Back on the material plane, Sam Xu was planning for the battle of his life as well. He had made himself a promise not to give up his fight until he had the identity and the address of the Quintus child within his grasp. It required long and tedious preparation but within weeks of his declaration of his intention to construct a new factory in America, steps had already been taken to finalize the purchase of the property for the building site. It was strategically located along the banks of Lake Erie. Sam had already concluded his negotiations with the construction firm that would erect his new building and thankfully Mrs. Xu was quite satisfied with the family's new home that she had chosen with the help of Sam's executive assistant. Samlin Xu was pleased.

"Everything is on schedule. All I need to worry about now is the education of my son," thought Sam, as he sat on the plane with his family and corporate officers in transit to America.

He pushed the intercom button on his desk in the office he had designed into his airplane and called to the outer room. "Please send the officer I have placed in charge of my son's education in America into my office immediately."

"Right away, sir," came the reply through the box.

"I am nearly there," said Sam to himself anxiously tapping his fingers on his desktop.

A few moments later, his office door opened and the requested officer entered.

"What news do you have for me?" Sam demanded.

"I have found, sir," the nervous officer began, "that the public school system in this area is comparable to our own public school system, if that is the path you should choose for your son."

"I was very specific that nothing but the best would be acceptable for my son. No public school is up to the task, not the one in our previous home and I will not consider the one associated with our new home. What other options have you discovered?"

"There is a thriving parochial and private school system in this area. I thought this possibility would be more of interest to you and I have made inquiries into it as well."

"Private education is more what I was looking for. Go on," Sam ordered.

"Yes, sir. I have compiled a list of the private schools in the area that have proven to consistently maintain the highest academic performance levels. But, you must know that there is an educational testing system also in place for all schools, public, parochial and private. This group must test young Master Xu before he can be placed in any school system."

"Use the air phone and see that arrangements are made for Po Duk to take these tests immediately."

"Of course, Mr. Xu. As you wish, sir." The officer left the room.

Mrs. Xu entered the office with tea for her husband. As she poured his cup she asked demurely, "Sam, I am most pleased with the pictures of our new house and I look forward to making it our family home. But I do not understand why it is that we had to move to a new country away from our family and friends."

Sam dreaded this moment. He had hoped she would never ask the reason but accept his decision, as was her duty. He could not fault her inquiry though, this was such a major change, and how could she not have some questions? He put his hand on hers and said gently, "I will tell you what I can, when I can, but for now, I need you to accept that this is our destiny."

Mrs. Xu looked at her husband with understanding and left the room.

The officer in charge of education returned. "I have made contact with the testing service as you ordered, sir. They are very excited about your relocation into their city and insist upon meeting you upon arrival. They plan to be at the airport tomorrow morning when we land. They will be waiting for you and have offered to provide transportation to your new home."

"Should I find that oddly generous?" inquired Sam, "or is this gesture merely the custom of the area?"

"I am uncertain, sir, however I believe there is a limited Asian presence in this region; and, if I may be so bold, you sir are an Asian of means and stature."

"And you think, they are somehow trying to use these facts to their benefit?" asked Sam.

"I do not know their motives, sir, mine was only a likely supposition." The officer in charge of education felt it necessary to qualify his statements.

"A reasonable one it is. I will keep it in mind." Sam saw relief cross the officer's face.

The next morning there was a man and woman waiting to greet them at the gate. They held a sign that simply read, 'Xu'. The man stood slightly in front of the woman. They thought Mr. Xu might be more comfortable if the man appeared to be in charge. This was the same pair that had gone to the La Roi home.

When the Xu party had deplaned and entered the gate area, the male of the pair stepped toward Sam and said, "It is my great privilege to welcome you and your family to America Mr. Xu. I am Frederick Piermont of the Educational Testing System of the Great Lakes Region. This is my colleague Ms. Truman." The woman beside him smiled demurely and bowed her head just a bit. He continued, "We would be most honored if you would allow us to provide you with transportation to your new home."

Sam looked them over for a few seconds. "Yes," he said, "that will be acceptable; however, I would like to speak with you in private. My corporate officers have arranged the transportation for my family. I, however, would be delighted to take you up on your offer. It will afford us the time to discuss matters of some urgency in private."

Once he was seated in the limousine with his two escorts, Sam continued their conversation. "I have great interest in my son's educational success." He began. "It is vital that he be the top student in any school he attends. May I count on you to point out the school best suited for our needs?"

"Of course, Mr. Xu," said the man. "We will have to test your son to find his strengths and weaknesses, but after those results are available, we will certainly be able to provide you with the best possible situation for his academic success."

"I am not certain you understand," Sam began. "My son's genius was without comparison in his former school system. I intend to assure him of the same standing in his new environment."

The woman, Ms. Truman, was reading through information in the file provided to her by the corporate officer in charge of Po Duk's education. "Oh yes, sir," she said with enthusiasm. "I can see that your son is tremendously gifted. In fact, we have only come across one other student that might closely resemble his ability. But she lives in another state and will in no way be in competition with Po Duk. Oh, and isn't this interesting," she showed the file to Mr. Piermont, "they were born on the very same day. Now that must have been a very lucky day."

Sam, smiled, a knowing smile, and took the folder from her hand and said, "Yes, it was a very lucky day indeed."

"Now, Mr. Xu, if you will allow us," Piermont interjected, "we would very much like to tell you about our programs for the extremely gifted, should Master Xu meet the criteria, of course."

"Oh, he will meet and surpass any requisite criteria," Sam said with pride as he read over the folder. "Of that you may be certain."

Section V: The Battles On Both Planes

I wasn't afraid of anything at the time. I really had no reason to be. I was totally unaware that Samlin Xu, an agent of Zank Xu himself, had discovered my name and address. It didn't matter at this point in my life story any way. Sam's knowledge of my personal information would not be useful to him until the second half of my grade school career. However, I did need to let you know how he came into possession of it. As this story continues, I found myself faced with the first time I was involved with a situation that was just wrong in my personal estimation and I chose to stand up and voice my opinion.

Chapter XXXI: The Fourth Grade Walkout

I had often thought of the advice given me by Dina, the friend Louise had brought with her to our visit. I had decided she made a great deal of sense. She said I didn't have to physically attack someone to make my point. I could use words to defeat them. And then it happened; the moment presented itself for me to act. I had to use my newfound confidence much sooner than anticipated, but I was ready and able to do my best. I mentioned earlier that my fourth grade class was the first class our teacher Miss Starling ever taught and that we were even her very first job right out of college. She proudly employed all the latest teaching techniques she had just learned. Many things were different from our first three years in grade school. In fact, Miss Starling thought even the design of the room and how the desks were situated was a vital part of our learning environment. Instead of having all of the desks in rows and columns and the teacher's desk at the front of the room, our classroom was set up with an equal number of desks on either side of a center aisle. Miss Starling liked to walk up and down the center aisle as she taught. That was, as she said, so every student would be focused on the center of the room where the teaching is going on.

I was seated in the front of my side of the room. I occupied the third desk in from the teacher's desk, which had been strategically placed in front of the windows. So instead of staring out the windows and day-dreaming when we wanted to, we had to look at the teacher, who would remind us to get back to work. The door or exit/entrance to the room was on the wall opposite the teacher's desk and window bank but the same wall as the chalkboards. It was to my left if I were facing the center aisle. There were fifteen students on each side, and rather than seating us alphabetically, as was the choice of previous instructors, we were seated according to our academic performance. A good student was on either side of someone who may be in need of help. We were placed five across and three rows deep. On my side of the room, I was front and center for everything.

Miss Starling had decided we should read *The Fourth Grade Nothing*, probably because we were in the fourth grade now. It was and interesting book. We each took turns reading aloud in class and would be stopped at passages Miss Starling thought relevant for class discussion. One day, while one of my classmates on the other side of the room was reading aloud, two boys in the third row on my side of the aisle were talking. They were in the back row so I couldn't tell who it was, but I could hear them talking. Miss Starling, who was pacing the center aisle, interrupted the reader and said, "One moment. Please excuse the rudeness of your classmates, Charla." She turned to my side and continued, "Is there something you gentlemen would like to share with the class?"

"No, Miss Starling," came from the back row.

"Then perhaps you would be good enough to provide your classmates the courtesy of your silence and attention while we discuss that passage that Charla just read?" Miss Starling asked sweetly.

"Yes, Miss Starling," came the simultaneous reply.

Miss Starling asked questions about what she considered to be a thought provoking passage from the book. And the two boys behind me started talking again.

"Well," she said as she turned and faced my side of the classroom. "Since the students on this side of the classroom cannot be respectful of their classmates or their teacher and remain silent unless appropriately participating in the discussion, I will only teach the students on the other side of the classroom who are cooperating and you will all receive zeroes for today's participation grade." With that she dramatically turned her back on everyone on my side of the aisle.

I heard protests from other students on my side of the room. "That's not fair."

"I was paying attention."

"But I wasn't talking."

"It's not my fault they were talking."

I felt my emotions steeling inside me again. This was truly an injustice and I was not going to stand for it. My courage was growing exponentially every second. I don't know where the words came from, but before I realized what was going on I was so full of righteous indignation that I was standing up next to my desk, and I said as loudly and as firmly as I could, "*My father pays tuition for me to attend this school. I did nothing wrong and do not deserve to have your back turned to me and I certainly do not deserve a zero for a participation grade. You are paid to teach all of us fairly and equally. How dare you turn your back on the rest of us who were trying to learn and were paying attention! If you are not going to teach me, then I will not stay here and be insulted and trivialized!*

With that final proclamation, I picked up my books, turned my back on Miss Starling and walked out into the hallway.

Within seconds, I heard my other classmates, even the cruel Lori Dizzertelli say, "She's right you guys, let's go!"

"We don't have to take this."

"My parents pay tuition and her salary too!"

"Wait until I tell my parents what you did, Miss Starling!"

"This is wrong of you, Miss Starling."

Every student on my side of the classroom picked up their books and walked out of the room to join me in the hallway. And then not all but several students from the other side followed right along.

"Wow! This is great!" I thought. "I stood up for myself and it worked! How cool is that?"

So there we were, most of the fourth grade class, standing out in the hallway. And then it occurred to me, "What do we do now?" I hadn't asked Dina or Louise for the next step. I was totally unprepared for the situation at hand or the consequences of my actions.

As a group of fourth graders, all full of righteous indignation, we were certain we were absolutely right in our course of action. I heard Gabriel, the most popular boy in class say, "Let's go to the office and report Miss Starling to Sister Benedictus for what she did!"

I heard another student say, "Yeah! Wait until Sister Benedictus finds out! Miss Starling will probably get fired!"

With no other ideas to go on, we turned as a group to walk down the hallway to the Principal's office when Sister Mary Benedictus, a rather large woman who looked like a linebacker to me, approached us from the opposite direction. She had an angry look on her face and a great deal of purpose in her stride. My classmates immediately shrunk and fell silent at the site of her. I found her a bit intimidating myself, but

I would not be deterred from my course of action. I hardened myself against her authoritarian presence.

"What are you children doing in this hallway?" came the deep voice of power and control in a nun's habit.

"Sister, Miss Starling turned her back on us and refused to teach us, so we left." I spoke up.

"Yeah, Sister, so we walked out because she's wrong!" Gabriel managed to sound a little tough but not really.

Even Lori Dizzertelli chimed in. "Our parents pay for us to go to school here, so she has to teach us. She can't give us all a zero for something we didn't do."

"Whose idea was this?" Sister asked in an accusatory tone.

Everyone turned and either pointed or looked at me. I heard a resounding, "*Jane!*" as a chorus from the crowd.

"Everyone *but* you, Jane, go back into your classroom and pay attention to and be respectful of your teacher. Jane, you will come with me," said Sister as if directing traffic.

I followed Sister down the hall and soon found myself sitting in a chair that was too big for me but still much smaller and shorter than hers opposite the elevated principal's desk. Sister Benedictus planted herself behind her large intimidating desk, in her large intimidating office.

"What was this all about Jane? You have always been such a quiet, respectful girl. You have never given us any trouble before."

"Miss Starling turned her back on everyone on my side of the classroom because two boys were talking quietly between themselves. Then she told us we would all get zeroes for today's participation grade because of their talking. That isn't right. The rest of us shouldn't be punished for something they did. I told Miss Starling that my father pays tuition for me to come to school here, so she should respect that and teach all of us fairly and that if she wasn't going to teach me then I wasn't going to stay there. What she did was wrong and I did the right thing by standing up to say so. I guess my classmates agreed with me because they got up and left too."

Sister Benedictus looked at me. She had to see the certainty of my belief written on my face. I was sure of it. She had to respect my righteous indignation and the action I took. She was going to tell me I had done a very brave and good thing and I was to be commended for standing up against injustice.

Only that's not what happened at all.

Sister Benedictus did not even hesitate a moment before she said, "You are a child! You do not tell a teacher what to do! You were disrespectful and caused a disruption not only in your classroom but also in the class across the hallway as well. You will go to the third grade room and apologize to Mrs. Frackle and her class for causing such a disturbance and then you will apologize to Miss Starling in front of your class for being disrespectful."

I was shocked. "But, Sister," I said, "I'm in the right and you know it. What she did was wrong! I'm supposed to stand up for what is right and that's what I did. Clearly the other kids thought so too!"

"That may be your perspective young lady, but it certainly is not mine, nor I suspect will it be your parents. You will do as you are told and that is final!"

"Well," I replied suddenly very calmly and in control, "I will apologize to Mrs. Frackle for disturbing her class. It isn't fair to them that Miss Starling's unjust actions caused a disruption in their class and they should not have to suffer for it. So, you are right, Sister, I will apologize to Mrs. Frackle and her class on behalf of Miss Starling. Although I do think it would be better if the apology came from Miss Starling herself as she is the root cause of the disruption." And then I looked Sister squarely in the eye and just as calmly said, "But I will *not* apologize to Miss Starling. She was wrong, I am clearly in the right and of this I am certain. This is an injustice and if you take Miss Starling's side then you are wrong too and just as guilty of that injustice." I got up and headed for the door. I liked this walking out tactic. It was really very dramatic and helped display the finality of my resolve.

"I will be calling your parents this evening, young lady. We will see what they have to say. I doubt your father will feel the same way you do."

Those were the words that trailed after me as I exited the office. She was wrong. She had to be.

CHAPTER XXXII: THE FALLOUT

I did go and apologize to Mrs. Frackle for the walk out incident and told her honestly that I'd hoped that Miss Starling's error in judgment did not cause too much of a disturbance in her class. Then I returned to my desk for the rest of the day. Miss Starling tried to act as if nothing had happened but I could tell she was shaken. I felt sort of bad about that. I did not like to hurt anyone's feelings. During math class, Sister Benedictus entered our classroom with Sister Mary Catherine.

"Sister Mary Catherine will be substituting for Miss Starling for a short while," Sister Benedictus announced. "I trust you will give her your full attention and respect."

"Yes, Sister Mary Benedictus," the class responded in unison. Sister Benedictus and Miss Starling left the room. We had Sister Mary Catherine for the rest of the day. I wondered what that meant.

I rode the bus home just like I always did. Josie actually sat down on the seat next to me.

"Spill it!" She ordered.

"What?" I asked. I didn't understand. I wasn't going to spill anything. I didn't even have anything open.

"Tell me what happened today," she demanded.

"Not too much," I said. "My teacher did something wrong and I told her it was wrong. That's all." No matter how much Josie prodded, I wasn't going to say anything more on the subject. I really did not think it was any of her business. We got off the bus and I thought we would walk to the house like always, but Josie sprinted ahead. I reached the breezeway and left my jacket and shoes in the appropriate place. Mom was standing at the kitchen sink peeling potatoes.

"Sister Mary Benedictus called today, Jane." Mom moved to the stove to continue making dinner. "She is very upset with how disrespectful you were to Miss Starling."

I tried out my newly found confidence on my mother. "I understand, Mom. But I am very upset with how disrespectful Miss Starling was to me and the other kids. How dare she turn her back on us and refuse to teach us? We didn't do anything wrong. Just because two boys were talking doesn't mean the rest of us should be treated badly. It wasn't right. Dad pays money for us to go to that school. It seems like the teachers ought to do what he's paying them for."

"What on earth made you think of walking out of your classroom?" Mom asked in exasperation.

I immediately realized that "what on earth" was the most important part of her question. I couldn't exactly tell my mother that a relative from the ethereal plane had visited me in my room the other night with a friend who told me all about protests and standing up for myself. Quickly, I thought of the strike my father, who was a Union Steward at his factory, had participated in last year.

"Remember last year when Dad and the other workers at the factory were unhappy with management, they walked out in protest and had a strike that lasted a week? Dad said they had to stand up and tell management they were wrong and that the workers were not going to take it anymore. Well, this was sort of the same thing. I stood up and told Miss Starling what she was doing was wrong and then I walked out. I had no idea the other kids were going to follow me. It just sort of happened."

"Your father is in the shed working on the tractor, and trying to cool off. You should go and do your homework before dinner. I believe he will have something to say to you soon enough."

"What do you mean 'cool off'? Why would Dad have to cool off?" I asked.

"Because he is very angry with your behavior." Mom was really trying to maintain her composure.

"But I was right and I was standing up for him. Why would my behavior make him angry?" I was really not happy with the direction this was going.

"Because, you are a child Jane and Miss Starling is an adult." Mom had said just about the same thing Sister Benedictus did.

"Why should chronology or body habitus have anything to do with what's right? She was wrong and I took appropriate corrective action. Where is the problem with that?" I was becoming upset myself.

"This is going to be a long conversation. Just go upstairs, change out of your uniform and start on your homework. You should make sure you get it all done before dinner. I would imagine your father has plans for you afterward."

"So I'm in trouble for doing the right thing? I don't get it." I stood there waiting for an explanation I could buy.

"Jane," Mom said in exhaustion, "go and do your homework, *please*."

I walked from the kitchen into the dining room where Josie had been listening.

"Jane's in trouble! Jane's in trouble!" she sang with true delight in her voice.

"Am not! You'll see! Dad will understand. Mom just doesn't get it," I spat back at her.

"Mom gets it, and you're really gonna get it!" She laughed as she ran upstairs to change her uniform to play clothes. "You're gonna get it!"

I went to my room and changed my clothes as instructed. My homework never really took very long. It was simply a matter of getting it done. It's not like I ever had to struggle with any of the concepts. It seemed like an interminable amount of time had passed, but finally, Mom sent out the call to come to the table for dinner. I found myself oddly nervous as I descended the staircase.

"Wash your hands girls," Mom called to us. "Josie, it is your turn to set the table."

We did as we were told. Our father and brother James were in the basement doing the same. Soon enough we were all seated around the kitchen table and Mom was filling plates with her hearty roast beef dinner.

"So, Jane," our father began, "I understand you caused some trouble at school today."

"I wasn't the cause of any trouble. Miss Starling was the cause," I replied quietly. I could see the look on Dad's face. It was the same look he had when James destroyed his last car. He was really not happy.

"Tell me what happened." He spoke with his "quiet authority" voice.

I took this as a good sign, because Dad never asked James or Josie for their side whenever they got into trouble at school. He always took the side of the teacher and proffered a punishment without any input from them. I dutifully repeated the story and was sure to include my righteous indignation while explaining how I was defending him and was totally in the right.

James snorted his milk through his nose because he was laughing and drinking at the same time.

"No, Jane, you may have been correct in your thoughts but your actions were very disrespectful. After you finish your chores, you will go to your room and you will write five thousand times, 'I will be respectful of my teacher.' You will not play or read until it is complete. Except for school, homework, chores and meals, you will be in your room writing this penalty until it is complete. Am I clear?"

"Yes, sir, but I was right; why do I have to write a penalty?" I asked in earnest.

"You were a disrespectful child and Miss Starling is an adult." Dad maintained his quiet authoritative demeanor.

"I don't understand what my age has to do with anything. I was in the right. Would someone please explain it to me so I can understand?" I really wanted an answer.

"You will understand some day. For right now, your job is to write the penalty. When the penalty is complete, you will take it to Miss Starling and you will ask her to sign it and then return it to me. This discussion is closed." Dad had made his final proclamation. I knew there would be no further debate.

Josie was practically beaming.

Chapter XXXIII: James Crashes

Having completed my punishment, I was now able to leave the house and resume my normal activities. So, when James offered to take me with him on an errand for Mom I jumped at the chance. I remember that James couldn't wait to drive. Even James's Christmas list the year he turned sixteen had only a single request; he wanted a car. My parents did, in fact, buy him a car that year. Only it was a matchbox car and they stuffed it in his stocking. James did not think the joke was funny, but everyone else seemed too. I asked him once why having a car was so important. He said that driving meant that he finally had some independence and a way off the farm, and out of our parents' sight. The only drawback was that he had to take the little sisters along sometimes. James said that was Mom's way of trying to keep him out of trouble and make him drive safely. I remember many conversations our parents had with James about his speeding tickets and the need for bodywork to his car. I gather he crashed a lot.

By forcing James to cart around a little sister Mom thought that if he did anything he wasn't supposed too, that Josie or I would be sure to tell her just as soon as we got home. What Mom didn't know is that James had worked out a deal with Josie that if she didn't tell Mom anything bad, he would buy her ice cream or some make up or something pretty for her hair. Josie saw what was in it for her and went along with the deal. I chose not to take the deal. I told James

I would not accept bribery but I also would not tell our parents anything unless I was asked a direct and specific question. I think my answer scared him a little bit because he didn't take me along as often as he took Josie. I only got to go on trips when there was absolutely no chance of any fun. That was the case this time too; we were just running to the post office to drop off a package for Mom.

James, of course, made it sound like he was doing Mom a favor.

"Sure, I'll take Jane with me." He told our mother, "It'll get her out of your hair for a while."

I know James was thinking he'd score some brownie points with Mom and, as a bonus when something fun did turn up, he could say, "I took Jane with me last time, to be fair I should take Josie with me this time." It was actually pretty good planning on his part if you ask me.

James made a show of making sure I was belted into the back seat and off we went into town. It was a nice enough drive on a beautiful day. The windows were down and the radio was blasting to Bob Seeger and the Silver Bullet Band. I sat in the back reading like always. I was tremendously happy. I felt free and alive and glad to be out of my room. James was talking to me about graduating high school and moving out. He loved to think about the future that was so close he could almost reach out and touch it. The future was definitely where his mind was when it happened.

I looked up from my book as saw another vehicle rapidly approaching the same intersection we were. It didn't slow down.

I screamed "*James!*"

In an instant there were tires screeching, glass breaking and a tremendous percussive impact. It felt like a bomb exploded right next to me. A pickup truck barreled through the intersection where we had the right of way. It didn't stop. It came out of nowhere and T-boned us. It was really crazy because I saw and heard everything happening in slow motion. The sound of metal shrieking, the feeling of being swatted aside like a rag doll, rolling over and over, glass breaking, my brother yelling and a horn blaring were all separate but simultaneous events.

We finally stopped rolling over and I thought I was okay. Thankfully, I had worn my seatbelt and so did James, probably because it wasn't Josie in the car with him. I heard him unbuckle and could hear him struggling to crawl out of the car. I couldn't understand why I couldn't see James. I couldn't see anything. James sounded like he was in a panic.

"Jane! Jane!" I heard him yelling. "You okay Jane?"

I couldn't respond. I couldn't move.

"Jane? "Jane!" James said louder each time. Still, I could not answer.

I tried desperately to free myself from my restraint. At least I thought I did. My hands and arms would not move. I heard a different voice at my window. It was a man's voice and one I did not know. I think he was kneeling on the ground next to my brother to see into the car.

"You okay, dude?" he asked. The smell of beer was heavy on his breath. "Sorry man, I didn't see ya."

"My sister, she's in the back!" James yelled frantically trying to unbuckle my seatbelt.

"Hold on, brother, I'll get her," he said as he pulled out a hunting knife from his boot and cut the strap on my belt. They pulled me out through the glassless window and laid me carefully on the side of the road.

"Dude! You got a nasty gash on your head!" I heard the other driver tell James.

"It doesn't matter," said James, "my sister isn't moving!"

I heard the whaling of a siren. Someone else had stopped and called for an ambulance. I was dizzy and feeling sick. James reached out and held my hand.

"It will be okay Jane; you just hang on," he said. That's the last thing of the accident I remember before waking up in the hospital.

Chapter XXXIV:
Jane Confronts the Council

I remember the truck coming at us. I remember seeing it hit us and I remember hearing the crumpling steel and breaking glass, but I don't really know what happened after the impact. I mean, I sort of do know, but not really. I think I opened my eyes for a brief moment. Everything was blurry. I heard a siren but it sounded like it was underwater. I saw a lady in a uniform with gloves on her hands looking at a cardiac monitor next to me. She smiled and said, "Everything is going to be alright, honey." Then everything went dark again.

The next thing I remember was some bright lights and lots of people wearing hospital protective gear bustling around me. Someone was cutting my pants. "No! Not my purple pants! Stop, I love these pants." I yelled it at the top of my lungs but no one stopped what they were doing. "Why won't anyone listen to me?" And then it occurred to me that maybe I didn't yell it at all; maybe I only thought it. Everything went dark again.

"Where am I?" I found myself standing in an empty seemingly limitless space. "Is anybody here? "Can anybody hear me?" I started to get scared but then I thought about Uncle Levi and the Council...and I started to get mad. "Now would be a good time to tell them how mad I am at them," I said to myself. "No one else is around so I think it's safe." I focused on the purple haze and created a slightly different version of the rhyme. I tried to control the anger in my voice hoping I wouldn't alert any one to how upset I was.

"I connect with thought of mind,
To ethereal beings beyond space and time.
I seek knowledge and wisdom,
Through the energy that binds,
And call to ancestors of the Quintus line.
Cross the veil and near me dwell,
I need Uncle Levi, Louise, and oh just give me the
whole Council as well!"

Suddenly, it seemed as if the swirls I had created in my head reached out and grabbed me. I was swept in through the purple misty haze right into the Council room. And there they were. Everyone looked very concerned.

"Okay, that was very cool," I said with amazement. And then I realized why I was there. "You guys got me into trouble," I said in an accusing tone.

Lucille spoke first. "Before we begin, we must apologize for causing of the trauma of the accident Jane. We needed to hold onto your consciousness for a little longer than our previous meeting. Your brother is fine and you will be too. Hopefully from this experience your brother James will understand the price that could be paid for driving recklessly. However, please know that it is necessary that you remain in an unconscious state on the physical plane for a short while. We need to speak with you at length without arousing the suspicions of your family.

"Wait," I said. "You caused the accident? How is that possible?"

Levi calmly answered my questions. "Time, as we have discussed, it is not linear for us, Jane, you know that. So, for your protection, we survey the possibilities of your immediate future through the view ports. We see what could happen and sometimes nudge the events one way or another. Take the accident, for example; the possibility existed that your vehicles would have a 'near miss' instead of a collision. So, to nudge the possibility of the accident Caroline used her energy to shift the flight of a hornet into the open window of the other driver. He was focused on the insect and not on the stop sign at that intersection where your paths crossed."

"But you could have gotten me killed! You could have killed my brother! How could you do that?" I was beyond exasperated.

"Nope. That wasn't in any one of the scenarios we saw," said Melvin. "And we ran it over and over again. We knew you'd be safe enough and your bother would be too. There's no way we'd have done it otherwise. C'mon, Jane, you have got to know that by now."

"I guess so," I said, but I was still a little mad.

"You see, Jane, there are very pressing matters to attend to," Lucille said calmly but firmly. "Tell Jane more of Zank Xu and of Po Duk Xu, Levi."

"Jane, you must listen carefully. This is so very important," Uncle Levi launched into lecture mode. "We have discovered that Zank Xu wishes to control not only his own destiny but also the destinies of each of the souls of the spirit clan of Xu. His great plan is to gain enough power in both realms so that he may know which spirits will be reincarnated at what times. He possesses his family members on the material plane in order to gain control of their assets and direct their circumstances. Xu can read the stars and the planets and energy fields. He devoted much time to the study of astrology while living on earth and has continued to study and chart while on the ethereal plane. We believe that he wants to decide who will be born at which time so that perhaps all his family will be born with great financial prowess or become charismatic leaders and gain power and therefore direct the path of the human lives and control what each soul has the capability and resources to learn. Can you imagine it? If that's not evil, I don't know what is."

"We believe a battle is coming, Jane," Gillius said dramatically. "This is not only our opinion it is also the opinion of all of your ancestors and we are sworn to stop Zank Xu in his quest for ultimate power."

"You have got to protect yourself, honey," Melvin said with grave concern. "If Xu gains influence over you on the material plane then he might be able to hold power over every one of us on the ethereal plane. See he would be able to use our own energy to bolster his strength against us."

"What? How can I protect myself if I don't even know what he looks like…in fact, how can I protect myself, anyway? What about my family? They don't know about any of this." I was becoming scared again.

Caroline said, "Don't worry; you will know him when you see him. We all just know him and his minions when they are around. It's sort of a gut feeling. You will recognize it immediately. Keep an eye out, if you see him or anyone from his family, you just send us a call and we will be right there, but we hope to handle it from this side." Caroline was standing now. It was like she was taking a stand against Zank Xu.

"We are all here for you precious," Louise tried to reassure me.

"Do not fret, young one," Jacob interjected. "We are already using Xu's own family members for information and actions against him.

There are not many, but a few, and one in particular, have been willing to brave the wrath of Zank Xu to aid us in our efforts."

"What remains for you to do, Miss Jane," I turned toward Melvin who was speaking, "is to go back to the material plane, wake up and be watchful. Here is the young man named Po Duk Xu." With a long sweeping motion of his arm, a vision of an Asian boy appeared in a view port in front of me. He had a high broad forehead and prominent cheeks. They were the kind that one of my aunt's would have pinched. I thought his chin was a little small for his face, but it wasn't terribly disproportionate. There was something about his eyes though; something that made me uneasy. They were black. At least that is how they appeared to me. I immediately corrected myself because I should not make any judgments based upon appearances. I told myself that was wrong.

"He doesn't look very dangerous," I said.

"And that is exactly why he is dangerous." Lucille was becoming a bit anxious, it seemed. "You must be on your guard at all times dear. If you see him you must walk away and call us."

"Alright, I will be careful and I will call for help if I need too. I promise," I said nervously.

Gillius stood. All members of the council immediately followed his action. They joined hands and closed their eyes and united their energies. The colors grew brighter and pulsated. The purple haze appeared and engulfed me quite suddenly.

I awoke in a hospital room, with my mother standing next to my bed.

"Hi, Mom," I said. "What's going on?"

"Oh, Jane!" My mother let out an emotional gasp. "You gave us such a fright!"

Chapter XXXV: The Battle for Eternity

The time has come to tell you of the Battle for Eternity, as my ethereal family calls their fight against Zank Xu. I suspect it's one of those family stories that gets bigger and bigger every time its told. And since it's going to be retold for eternity, I thought I should relate it now before a later and much bigger version develops.

The forces of Zank Xu began to amass outside the energy barrier of the St. John estate. The alarm was sounded by the lookout posted atop the stonewall.

"They are coming! They are coming!" He blew several blasts on a loud horn to warn those preparing the grounds.

The sound of the horn alerted Sir Orville who waved his hand and opened a view port to see across the energy barrier more clearly. There were hundreds, no thousands, of troops all dressed in the battle gear of the time Zank Xu lived on the material plane. They came in droves, marching side by side.

"Well," said Sir Orville to himself, "this may be a shorter battle than we had envisioned, but we will make it a hard fought one!" He closed his eyes and focused his thoughts. "Gillius, I do hope your plan is already put into action. Now would be a righteous time indeed. We are significantly outnumbered." Then he summoned the squire who helped him don his armor.

The Legion of St. John had prepared for the barriers emanate failure. Now all that remained was to take up battle positions. Some soldiers positioned vats of energy sapper high on the castle walls to rain down on Xu's men. Others stocked, sited and loaded the catapult with great bags of the same solution bursting at the seams.

Xu's army had situated a cannon to send his own special energy-draining potion toward the barrier protecting the St. John estate. Once the cannon was in place, Zank Xu himself wearing the battle armor of the highest generals of his time, with a few extra shiny embellishments on the wrist cuffs and chest plate (to make him appear more impressive, of course) entered the scene dramatically, with ostentation and pomp. Great lines of battle drummers pounded their instruments in a terrifying beat to signal his presence. His giant white stallion was girded in gilded bridle and bit. His saddle and his armor carried the golden crest of his family or rather of him. There were huge black flags also bearing his golden coat of arms that marched before and behind him.

Zank Xu stood in the stirrups to appear even taller than he already was and announced loudly, "Those who would defy me will be imprisoned and become slaves in my empire. However, so that you may know of my benevolence, I generously give you a single opportunity to dispel my former first advisor from your property and ally with my family."

Lord Bernum had joined his brother in the armory to don his battle gear as well.

"Make certain, Cong Ming, the women and children are safe in the keep before you join me in the Inner Ward, will you brother?" asked Sir Orville.

"Of that you may be absolutely certain," Bernum replied. "I will also send someone to check the Postern gate, as I have not yet heard any sounds of alarm from there. I wish to be certain Xu has not employed a sneak attack from the rear and already overcome our soldiers stationed there. You do not suppose that Xu could be so arrogant as to attack from the front only, do you?" Lord Bernum said with hopeful incredulity.

Sir Orville laughed. "With an ego the size of the universe as he has, I shouldn't doubt it for a moment. Besides, I do not believe he has any real battlefield experience. His wars were all fought with money. But yes, definitely check the rear, just in case he is not fighting with only his ego but has brought a few wits along with him too."

Back in front of the energy barrier, Zank Xu was becoming visibly angry at the defiance of the St. John family who, had failed to immediately and unconditionally surrender to his greatness.

Shaking his fist at the great barrier, he screamed, "You will long regret your inaction and not accepting my most charitable offer!" Crazed with anger, to his army he roared, "*Fire! Fire!* Fire, you imbeciles! *Fire!*"

The cannon boomed repeatedly; each time it was repositioned to target the energy barrier protecting the St. John estate.

As the barrier began to weaken, the soldiers of St. John shot arrows and catapulted skins of their own energy sapping soup toward and through the barrier at Xu's army. It was a fierce battle.

The warriors of Zank Xu stood at the ready with their swords drawn. They would attack once the barrier was completely ineffective. They were determined not to fail their master, but they were scared. Some of their comrades had already fallen victim to the arrows and catapulted skins. Two of Xu's men attempted to remove their fallen from the front lines of the battle. When they examined the seemingly lifeless beings they realized they were not injured at all. The wounded soldiers were merely sleeping.

One warrior said to the other next to him, "If we allow ourselves to be captured by the St. John family, we may have better lives in their prison than we do in our master's realm."

At that moment Zank Xu issued the command, "Leave them! Leave them! When we advance on the castle, you will simply march over them!"

"Yes, Master!" the two replied and immediately rejoined their lines. Each of them spread the information they had to other warriors around them. The plan spread like fire. Soon several warriors had overheard the comments and started to run toward the arrows and flying skins of sleeping solution. They charged the energy barrier with everything they had in them. Some began to fight each other to be the first through the gateway. Each was desperately hoping to be struck down by an arrow or to have even the smallest drop of solution fall on him.

"Such a tremendous leader am I that my family cannot wait to sacrifice themselves to further my greatness," Zank Xu proudly proclaimed to his second advisor who was standing next to his horse. "This surprises me a bit, but of course it shouldn't. In my perfect world, this is exactly how I have envisioned it should be. I took a vow that I would regain my power and control and now I have realized that goal. Look at how devoted my warriors are. I must remember to allow each one who sacrifices himself an extra scrap of energy from my table."

Xu was focused on the battle raging in front of him as his lines continued to move forward toward the castle. He was so engrossed in the devotion of his warriors that he missed the advancement of Melvin and his troops from the rear. Melvin, who created the attack plan, had with him every family member and friend of the family who had ever served in any form of military service. Each veteran was wearing the battle dress of his own war. They outnumbered the warriors of Zank

Xu by thousands, but their approach was so quiet their presence went unnoticed.

Lord Bernum joined Sir Orville in the inner ward. "I cannot believe the foolishness of this idiot soul. He truly is attacking only from the front. The rear is secure and so are the women, children and Cong Ming."

"You are right on time, brother, Gillius' family has just now arrived, the battle is truly about to begin.

Arm yourselves!" Sir Orville shouted to all his family fighters positioned behind him as he mounted his steed. "Lower the drawbridge!" he yelled to the gatekeepers.

The clanking of the chains straining against the weight of the great drawbridge filled the atmosphere.

"*Attack!*" ordered Sir Orville as he led his men charging over the bridge, to meet their opponents on the battlefield.

Horns and trumpets blared, battle flags whipped in the wind while horses whinnied and soldiers yelled battle cries with fierce rage. Great angry clouds of dust announced their furious advance. Zank Xu was caught off guard; he had anticipated a fight, but not one with such fervor.

From the left flank came Gillius Quintus dressed in the armor of a roman general. With him were hundreds of thousands of ancient warriors of different types and origins. There were Greeks, Romans, and Vikings. All were family members and friends of the Quintus family.

Over a hill from the right flank Jacob and Caroline lead legions of settlers and Indians. There were some from early America and other from the American westward expansion. Some of their battalion members were the settlers of Mexico and the Mexican army who fought at the Alamo; still others were mountain men and those who died during the California gold rush.

Gillius gave the order to advance. "*Incursus!*"

"What are they doing?" Zank Xu was curious at first. All of the fighters with the Quintus family moved forward. "Could they actually be trying to attack me? Could they really be that insolent? Cannot they see how devoted my men are that they rush in despite the arrows to serve me?"

Anxiety suddenly overcame him. In his mind he flashed back to the forced march that had taken his family. "I will not lose my power again! I cannot!

First!" he screamed to his first advisor. "Quickly, move three battalions to the rear! *Third!* Redeploy your men to the right flank! Second! You must take command of those battalions," he said, pointing to the group he wanted to move, "and protect my left flank! *Move! Move!*"

The advisors did as they were charged and repositioned Xu's army. The end result was a perimeter of security with Zank Xu squarely in the center.

The odds were overwhelming and Xu's warriors were scared to move against the Quintus soldiers, but they were much more frightened of Xu. They held their positions, unable to move forward or retreat.

Gillius saw their dilemma. He was unwilling to harm them unnecessarily. After all, they had absolutely no control over the family they had been born into. He raised his right hand so all of his soldiers could see and said, "*Concesso!*"

They stopped immediately.

Xu's men were not certain what to do. They froze for just a moment.

"*Fight! Fight! Fight!* You imbeciles!" an enraged, or perhaps scared, Zank Xu ordered.

Suddenly from the wall walk of the castle came a voice. It was very loud and very clear. "Stop! Stop! My family, I beg you to stop your attack!"

The warriors of Xu stopped dead in their tracks and looked up to the top of the wall surrounding the estate. To their great surprise speaking to them was Cong Ming, the former first. He was strong (no doubt, thanks to Nora's pudding) and unafraid.

"We must not fight any longer. These are good, kind and generous souls. They have taken me into their home and cared for me. Their actions have reminded me of what it really means to be a family. I beg you, my brothers, listen to me."

"There you are, you traitor! You will come down from that wall and prostrate yourself before me this instant!" ordered Zank Xu.

Cong Ming looked down at him with pity. "I will not," he said almost matter-of-factly. "I have suffered at your whim long enough." Louder he said, "We have all suffered by your will long enough. You take our energy for your own purpose; you torture us and force us to live in hovels. You compel us to exist by your rules. No longer will I live in this manner."

Zank Xu was insanely furious. "You forget your place, former first!" he bellowed.

"My name is *Cong Ming*." He stood taller.

The Lady Nora had been watching and clapped with joy. "You tell them Mingy!" she said with encouragement.

Cong Ming continued to address his family members. "We must stand against this injustice! If we band our energy together and turn our backs on Zank Xu, he can have no power over us."

There was silence for a moment.

The second advisor pulled together every ounce of courage he had, stepped forward and addressed Zank Xu. "Your men, as you call them, were not trying to serve you, as you thought They were trying to escape from you! They hoped to be hit by the energy sapping solution of the St. John army so they could be taken prisoner! Look around you. Can you not see the breadth and depth not only of the Quintus family but also of their unending connections? *They* have friends across eternity; you have only servants. Who is it you think will win this battle?"

The warriors of Zank Xu all turned and faced him with their weapons at the ready.

Cong Ming spoke again. "If we take our vengeance this way then we will remain his victims forever. If I have learned anything during my stay with the St. John family, it is that fairness, putting family first and doing what is right are always much better arbiters of justice. If we treat him the way he treated us, we are no better than he." The Xu clan and everyone with the Quintus family were listening in earnest. "We cannot destroy his energy; that is not within our capability. But eternity is not without justice. Why not help the soul of Zank Xu see the errors of his chosen path by keeping him an eternal prisoner? We can use the energy sapping potion he had loaded into his horrible cannon against him to keep him imprisoned until it is his time to be reborn."

A loud raucous cheer went up from the warrior masses.

It was only then that Zank Xu realized he was outnumbered by hundreds of thousands from all sides. They were all against him. His men included. Suddenly, he felt quite vulnerable. But he would not lose control, he would not lose power, he had sworn his soul to it. So he gave more orders. This time he stood in the stirrups of his saddle to be certain all of his men could see and hear him.

"You will not dare defy me!" He shook his fist at Cong Ming as he said it. Those were the last words heard from Zank Xu that day.

It was then that Melvin took aim with his rifle and shot Zank Xu in the butt cheek with a bullet coated with sleeping solution. Zank Xu fell ingloriously and awkwardly to the ground. One foot still stuck in its stirrup. His warriors gasped when they realized their master was not only asleep but for the moment also at their mercy.

Melvin waved to Cong Ming. "I am sorry, sir," he said loudly for all to hear. "But I just can't cotton to another word from that man's mouth. Someone needed to shut it for him."

The warriors of Xu turned with the speed of a pack of wolves and attacked him with the vengeance of their collective anger at how they had been treated.

"Stop! Stop! I beg you my family, *stop!* Violence is not the answer." Cong Ming was pleading with his family from the castle wall.

They stopped their assault and looked up at Cong Ming.

The *now former* second shouted. "We need a new leader but none of us have the experience of true family bonds. You have lived with a family who put everything on the line to protect you. We don't know what that is like. Would you lead us and teach us what you have learned?"

A great cheer went up again from the hundreds of thousands who came to battle with Gillius, Melvin, Jacob and Caroline. It was Gillius who spoke.

"Tell us, sir, what is it that you have learned?"

After thinking briefly, the Cong Ming replied with authority, "My name is Cong Ming. I have value in who I am and in who I will become. We need to lean on each other to build relationships and cooperate to grow and learn. We must stand up against injustice without violence if possible. We each have a name and we should use it. If I am to lead this family, then I have this requirement: All members of the Xu clan must work together to rebuild our family; to repeal the damage done by our former master; and to grow as a family."

An uproarious cheer came from all members of all families.

Sir Orville addressed Cong Ming and his family. "It would be my honor, sir, to help you and your family as Gillius Quintus and his family did for us. We will show you how to make an energy building pudding and to create true homes for yourselves. But first, and most importantly, allow us to take care of your most pressing difficulty." Sir Orville motioned to two of his soldiers who dragged Zank Xu off to his prison cell under the castle.

"We are most grateful to you and your family Sir Orville, and to all of you in the Quintus family. We will never be able to repay your kindness." Cong Ming bowed in respect as he spoke.

"There is no need for repayment sir," Sir Orville replied. "The same aid was given my family when we were overtaken by dire circumstance. You need only do the same for another family when and if you are able."

There was music, dancing and a great feast in the castle that evening…after all, Lady Nora had great vats of pudding and somehow they had to awaken the warriors sleeping on the battlefield. The celebration went on and on for what seemed an eternity.

Epilogue

Chapter XXXVI: Jane Crosses Paths With Po Duk

I was summoned to the Council room once more that year. It was just the same as the first time I visited them. Uncle Levi came to me while I was asleep and escorted me over to the ethereal side of life. They were so happy to tell me of the defeat of Zank Xu. And honestly, I was truly relieved to hear it. It felt good to feel safe again. I mean really, what could I ever have done against an evil malicious entity that could control people here on the physical world? Yes, I was definitely relieved. I went through the rest of the school year without any additional drama or difficulty. I had made a few more friends and had earned the respect of the "popular" kids by unintentionally leading the walk out. So it seemed to me that everything was okay and life was pretty good. Still, I was grateful the fourth grade was over. Next year was the fifth grade and a move up to the "big kids hallway". That was the long hallway that ran between the fifth through eighth grade classrooms. Somehow I felt that moving into that side of the building would make a difference.

Uncle Levi and I had scheduled regular meeting times so my education could continue. These lectures were actually the highlight of my day. I was always happy to talk and listen to Uncle Levi. Louise, Lucille and Caroline were pleased to answer any "girl" questions I might ask and Melvin and Jacob were really helpful on family camping trips. They taught a lot about making a fire and building a shelter and plant and animal life in the woods. In fact, my daily life was going along so well, I had no reason to take notice of the Asian family that moved into the city just over the line in the next state. We didn't go to town that often and their kid went to a wealthy private school, so it was unlikely that our paths would ever cross…until they did.

Mom signed Josie and me up for art lessons at the Toledo Museum of Art on Saturdays during the summer. She was intent on making us aware of culture and of expanding our interests in the arts because, as she said, we might not always live on the farm. I liked some of these classes like pottery and etching but some I really didn't care for, like drawing. I had absolutely no talent for it and wasn't interested in developing it. The best part of this sort of training was the tour we would go on of the museum as part of the lesson. The instructor would use an artist's actual work to show us what he or she was attempting to teach.

One Saturday, I was particularly pleased because we were going to spend the class in the ancient Egypt section. This was my favorite part of the whole museum. As my class entered the mummy exhibit to study the drawings of ancient Egypt, I got a disturbingly sickening feeling in my gut and I remembered the words Caroline had told me when I was in the council room after the accident: "We all just know him and his minions when they are around. It's sort of a gut feeling. You will recognize it immediately." I looked around the room but didn't see any one. "Well of course you don't see anyone dummy," I reproached myself for my silliness. "The Council told you that Zank Xu was in prison. What are you thinking?" I was wholly disappointed in myself for letting my imagination run away with me. I was much too much a realist for that. Still, I could not shake that sick feeling in my stomach and the dread that accompanied it. I found myself searching every nook and cranny of the room instead of listening to the teacher's presentation. I was glad when we were told to return to our classroom in the basement. "Good," I thought. "This room is really getting to me."

The group gathered by the sign designating the exit of the Egyptian room and walked single file into the next area of the museum. We passed through that room and into a connecting corridor and there he stood right by the fire alarm. It was as if that red emergency box was an indicator of the presence of Po Duk Xu. He recognized me and I him instantly. We locked eyes and just stared at each other. It was like we stared into each other's soul. I don't know what he saw when he looked at me, but I thought I saw something that looked like a dark cloud hovering behind him.

He nodded to me. I wasn't going to be intimidated so I gave him a single nod back. My teacher began to speak again and I forced myself to turn and pay attention. I acted as if his presence did not disturb me at all but nothing could have been farther from the truth. Thankfully, the class moved onto another room and I followed along feeling his cold icy stare piercing my spine. "Just keep going," I told myself, "keep going and don't look back."

To be continued.

CPSIA information can be obtained at www.ICGtesting.com
Printed in the USA
BVOW041317311212
308874BV00008B/2/P